CRUEL LOVE

A DARK COLLEGE SPORTS ROMANCE

HIDDEN VALLEY ELITE
BOOK SIX

ISLA VAUGHN

ARROWSCOPE PRESS, LLC

(p) ISBN-13: 978-1-951919-51-1

(e) ISBN-13: 978-1-951919-50-4

Publisher: Arrowscope Press, LLC; www.arrowscopepress.com

Editing— Kate B., Line Editor, Libybet R. G., Proofreader, Angie G., Red Adept Editing

Cover Design—T.E. Black Designs; www.teblackdesigns.com

Interior Formatting & Design— Arrowscope Press, LLC; www.arrowscope-press.com

CHAPTER ONE

PHOENIX

I couldn't escape. In one second, everything had gone pitch-black, and I floated in a void. I recovered there, in that dark sea of nothingness. It never lasted long before I returned to the same recurring nightmare that played on a constant loop. My mind and body were exhausted as I fought on repeat against multiple factors for survival.

The void only lasted so long before I was torn from it and returned to the open-top Jeep with no front doors. My brother, Shane, occupied the passenger seat. I sat behind the driver, and to my right was a girl with sun-bleached blond hair. No matter how hard I tried, I could never see her face.

I tried to place her among the people I knew but never could. And for a few brief seconds, my gaze locked on my brother. It was coming. I braced myself for the first impact, for that initial terrible crunch of metal.

One minute, Shane was there. In the next, he was gone. But the connection between us remained. My twin lived. I didn't know where he was, but he was still tethered to me.

Before I could question anything else, my instincts took over, and I grabbed the blond girl, wrenching her close and covering her with my body. I wrapped my forearms around the top of her head, tucking her tightly between me and the length of the rear seat.

Then the next hit came and another as the vehicle spun with dizzying speed. Pain exploded in my head. Then I returned to the void.

There were no answers, but as I floated in the darkness, it didn't matter. The nightmare slipped away, and I could rest.

I'd lost count of how many times the cycle repeated itself, but one day, it changed. Faint whispers reached me below the murky darkness, pulling me. I fought with everything I had to swim to the surface. My body was heavy and slow to respond. It felt like someone else's, which only made me more determined to free myself.

What awaited beyond my heavy eyelids and the depths of that void? The push and pull went on for far too long. And as I got closer to what I knew was the surface, my other senses kicked in. Something was off. I didn't recognize the sounds or the smells.

With a final push, I broke free. Everything was different in this new state of being. My body was heavy and tired, and a shockingly bright light shone like the sun through my closed eyelids. *Where the hell am I?*

It had to be the football field. Nothing else made sense. But then the struggle to stay conscious proved too much, and I drifted back under but nowhere near as deep as before.

The beeping, which didn't sound like the alarm on my phone, didn't pull me out of my deep sleep, but somewhere in my brain, the familiar scent of strawberries and vanilla teased me with an annoyingly out-of-grasp memory. The smell pushed past the ever-present one of disinfectant, which I recognized from visiting Mom at work in the hospital a long time ago.

The soft murmur of voices volleyed over me. I recognized one as Mom's, but the other... I couldn't place it. My mind and body were lethargic and heavy. I fought to open my eyes as I swam through a deep, dark body of water. It was calm there, and I struggled to leave it. But something inside me strained to reach that familiar scent that I knew was tied to the voice I couldn't place.

With effort, I pried open my heavy eyelids. Shards of pain accompanied the light piercing the darkness, and I immediately shut them again. After three more tries, I kept them partially open, finally able to endure the overhead glare. I held still, waiting for the fog to clear before alerting anyone that I was awake. I needed a moment.

Mom clung to one hand, and someone else held the other. It would have been weird for Shane, so I figured it wasn't him. I looked right to see who it was, trying to ignore how my badly head throbbed. I must have taken a massive hit in the game.

But it was even worse than that, I realized as I blinked a few times. *What is going on?*

No one noticed I was awake, giving me a few moments to acclimate. A girl held my other hand, and I worked to bring her blurry face into focus. After a few seconds of concentrating, I could see better. *Damn, she's hot. But older, like, in college. Why is she holding my hand?*

Sun-kissed blond hair fell in waves around her shoulders. She had blue eyes the color of the sky, a stop-in-your-tracks face, and skin that glowed. She was gorgeous and looked like she should be at the beach, probably more at home on a surfboard than she was sitting inside some stuffy hospital room.

Because that's where I was. From my angle, all I could see were the white bedsheet, blank walls, bed rails, and blinking machines, but it was enough. An IV was in my arm. I wanted pull it out, but moving my other hand was too much effort. I was worn out, and everything felt heavy. The will to keep my eyes half-mast took a massive amount of effort. *Maybe there's something else in that IV besides fluids. Bet they're giving me a muscle relaxer or something to make me this tired.*

I must've gotten sacked way harder than I'd thought. I would let the offensive line have it when I got out of here. They had to do a better job. I'd busted my ass to get us to the championship, and they needed to step up and hold the line, or Fenley would lead the team. No one wanted that. The second-string quarterback was mediocre at best.

I studied the hot girl, trying to figure out why she was touching me. She had worry written all over her face, but she couldn't have been my girlfriend. She was obviously in college. *I mean, I'd do her, but I can't date someone that much older than me.* I pulled my hand away and looked at my mom.

"Phoenix?" Mom's voice was full of emotion, and she squeezed me tighter. Then she was on her feet, kissing my face and crying in front of the hot girl.

"Mom," I croaked. Damn, I was thirsty. And my throat felt like it'd been shredded. *What did they do, shove a tube down it?*

She wiped the tears running down her face then gave me a shaky smile that I knew was supposed to be reassuring, but it wasn't. The tears kept falling. I didn't like it. I tried to talk, to tell her I was okay and that it had only been a brutal hit from the game, but the words wouldn't come out. I just croaked. Nothing made sense.

"Oh, here, honey." She sniffled, grabbed a cup with a straw from the tray, and held it to my lips.

The whole damn thing was embarrassing. I tried to tell her to stop, but fuck it. I sucked down the water.

"Slow down, Phoenix," Mom ordered before taking the drink away.

"Why am I in a hospital? And where's Shane?"

"Shane is in class right now." She gripped my hand again. "He'll be by later."

"What happened?" *This is so weird. Since when do we call being at school being "in class"?*

"Can you tell me the last thing you remember?"

"We were playing in the state championships. That monster defensive end broke through the line. I took that hard hit. Why? Did he hit me again? Fucking Jones. He's let too many through the line. Is that why I'm here?"

Mom obviously tried not to look concerned, but she was shit at hiding her feelings. A spike of alarm shot through me. *What isn't she telling me?* I turned to the blond surfer girl standing over me. I still didn't know who she was. I almost asked, but I had a feeling I might blurt out something about all the different ways I would fuck her, and I sure as hell didn't want my mom to know about it. But the girl made me hard, and that was going to give me away.

Mom hit the call button, and a doctor in a white lab coat walked in. He looked like a tool, and I wanted to smirk, but damn, I was super tired, and I'd just woken up. This day was out of control.

The tool introduced himself as Dr. Stevens. I said hi but could barely pay attention. It was either sleep to talk to the girl. That was all I was interested in.

"Can you tell me your name?"

I smirked. "Phoenix Bennet."

"Good. And your age?"

Not cool, doc. "Fourteen."

Mom froze. She had been fussing with all the cords on my bed, moving the remote closer to me. The color drained from her face, and I watched her as the doc asked me more stupid questions, like "Who's the president?" and "What year is it?" She started crying again, and the doc motioned for her to follow him into the hallway.

I was alone with the chick and had no idea who she was.

CHAPTER TWO

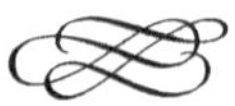

ASPEN

"Fourteen, Max." Panic swirled around me in frantic swarms of chaotic energy. "Phoenix thinks he's fourteen fucking years old and still in high school. He's explained the injury as being from a helmet-to-helmet hit he took at the state championship game that knocked him out, saying that's why he's in the hospital."

Max sat on a pink-and-silver beach towel while I paced the sand in my pink bikini, fiddling with the waistband of the white wrap I'd tied low around my hips. The beach was the one place where I felt at peace, where there were no worries too great. But this… I couldn't understand what was happening and why.

"He's only been awake for a couple of days," Max said. He was right, and I knew that his brain might still have been healing, but the accident had been more than a month ago. How long does it take a brain to heal?

"It's not okay. I mean, I'm glad he's awake, but not remembering… it's unreasonable." I yanked my hair out of its messy bun and scrubbed the pads of my fingers against my scalp in a desperate attempt to ease some tension. "He doesn't know who I am or that I'm carrying his baby."

Max crossed one leg over the other at the ankles and frowned. Thick strands of his dark hair danced in the wind before he smoothed it back. "Do you think he's faking it? And maybe for the lamest way possible… trying to get out of being a dad?"

I plopped down next to Max on the beach towel and hugged my knees to my chest. Resting the side of my face on top of them, I regarded his perplexed expression. "I'm pretty sure he's legit screwed up." That left me in a weird place. I was fine raising our kid myself, but… "His mom knows about the baby. There's no way I can fake that to her. She's a nurse, and she saw the chart, but it doesn't say who the dad is, so at least there's that. Then my dad freaked out."

"What do you mean?" Max squinted. "What did he do?"

A pit settled in my stomach. "After he found out I was okay, aside from minor bruises, the nurse opened her big mouth."

"Mentioned the baby?"

"Yeah." I dug my heels into the sand. "He was already wound tight about the entire situation. When she said the baby was unharmed, he freaked. Stepped back and hit one of those metal trays the nurse had set up. It tipped, and stuff clattered everywhere. I think he was embarrassed, and that only fueled the word salad that came out of his mouth when he said I'd survived a potentially fatal car accident but emerged with my problem intact."

Max's mouth formed an O. "Oh, wow. He didn't."

"I told him to get out." I swiped at the stupid tear that dared to roll down my cheek. "Mom got in the middle, and it turned into one of their epic arguments but in the hospital with witnesses rather than at home."

He cringed. "I'm afraid to ask who heard."

"You should be." I blew out a breath. "Phoenix's mom was in the hallway. She paused at my door."

"Did your dad say it was Phoenix's baby?"

"No. She knows I'm pregnant, though. If not from my dad's big mouth, then from my chart."

"She doesn't work there, though."

"Doesn't matter. She talked with the nurses and doctors and checked on me. I'm sure she knows. We don't touch that subject, so maybe she doesn't know it's her son's baby."

"One good thing, I guess." Max threaded his fingers through mine.

"Then Mom"—this part was so weird—"defended him. Said some stuff about him being under a tremendous amount of stress at work. Like that makes it all okay."

"You're the scapegoat. Lucky you."

"Yeah, lucky me." I was done. I didn't want to rehash that colossal nightmare anymore. "Anyway, it was a big scene."

"I'm sorry, baby girl." Max raised an arm, making room for me. "Come here."

I scooted closer and leaned against his side, contemplating the situation. I liked Phoenix's mom a lot. She was kind and patient. Not once had she made me feel less than others or seemed like she thought I was trying to take advantage of her son—not that I'd admitted I was carrying his kid. She didn't ask, but I swore she knew. She also kept me updated on his progress and asked about mine, making sure I knew she was available should I need anything.

"Have the headaches stopped?"

"No." We'd taken a massive hit in the car accident. "But I feel normal otherwise. And the baby's okay."

"I'm not surprised about that. From what you said, Phoenix saved you, shielded you with his body."

Aside from the horrific accident, it was the stuff of dreams. Heroic and protective, he had sacrificed his safety for mine and our unborn child's. "Shane was so lucky he was thrown from the car." If he hadn't been, he wouldn't have survived. The front end and side where he was sitting were crushed. I'd been tucked securely under Phoenix, but the door had rammed into his head from the force of impact against another vehicle. Shane had landed on the hood of a sedan, and their dad was partially thrown out of the car through the windshield. Both had sustained contusions but nothing too severe. It was nothing shy of miraculous.

"Is your dad talking to you yet?"

Speaking of dads. "No, not after making sure I was okay when I was in the hospital last month after the accident. He can't let it go that I got knocked up."

"I don't get it. You're self-reliant, still in school, and starting your own business. What's not to be proud of? He needs to get over his shit."

I agreed, but I also understood, in a way. "He's hurt. He wanted better for me than he could give Mom, my sister, and me." I hadn't known the extent of his feelings until Mom explained it at the hospital. Once he knew I was okay, Dad didn't visit. I got my stubbornness from him.

We fell into a companionable silence, and I rested my head on his shoulder. Each of us stayed lost in our thoughts as waves broke along the shoreline. The sun was high in the sky, and I was beginning to think about lunch. I wanted to surf a little more before we headed back to hit the cafeteria. I wasn't a huge fan of cafeteria food, but I'd paid for it and was going to use my meal plan until I had to move out. Even with my part time job at the diner, I couldn't swing living on campus next semester.

Phoenix had been giving me envelopes of money he earned from the underground fights. The last event—the fight he'd lost —had been on the night of the accident. I hadn't touched any of the money. I couldn't use it. Nothing about it felt right, so I opened a savings account for the baby. It would be her money someday, a gift from her dad. And if she never got to know him as her father, then there would be even more meaning behind it. Because before the amnesia, when he knew who I was and how she'd come to be, I knew he would have given her the world.

Max squeezed my shoulder. He'd come along to make sure I was safe while surfing, which was where I found solace. Knowing how important it was to me, the doc said it was fine as long as I wasn't careless. My friends and I had a group chat set up so that someone could be with me if I wanted to go. Even more than before, lately, I wanted to lose myself in the waves every spare moment I got.

"Are you going to go back to the hospital?"

I sighed. Phoenix was all we'd talked about, and a part of me couldn't forget how I'd taken advantage of my friendship with Max, making everything about me. "I'm probably not going to go back. He doesn't remember me, anyway." That was hard to admit. "The doctor has no idea if he'll get his memory back." I gestured at my belly. "And I'm showing and don't want to spring it on him." I wouldn't mind seeing him again, especially after the way he'd protected us that night.

After the accident, I'd taken a long, hard look at our situation and stopped being stubborn. I had feelings for Phoenix. It had hit me like a Mack truck one day as I sat at the hospital and talked to his mom, listening to her tell stories about Phoenix when he was young and how he'd struggled knowing his dad abandoned them. The stories she told showed me how tough he was and how he tried to protect everyone he cared for.

"Maybe Phoenix not remembering is a good thing. You can help him remove his head from his ass so he can be a part of the baby's life."

Max wasn't Phoenix's biggest fan, beyond enjoying what a smoke-show he was—those were Max's words. But he wasn't wrong.

I would have liked for him to be part of the baby's life and not get in his own way with his attitude, but I wasn't going to push. The thing was, I never really had him in the first place.

We'd shared one explosive night at the cove last July, resulting in my getting pregnant, and then we'd tried to be fake boyfriend and girlfriend, but that had been full of misunderstandings and hurt feelings.

So no, I wouldn't try to make him remember or be a part of our lives. Even if it meant I lost him for good.

CHAPTER THREE

PHOENIX

Holy shit! Shane is huge! Built like a truck and fucking old!

"It's because we're nineteen and in college now." My brother held my gaze without flinching.

The evidence was right in front of me but still so hard to believe. We had just been at the state championship game, freshman year of high school. I struggled to understand how I'd lost five years of my life. I couldn't figure out how to wrap my head around it. I had so many questions.

Pain sliced through my temples like someone was trying to split my head open with a knife. I pushed the heels of my hands to my forehead, desperate to stop the agony that hit me every time I attempted to understand, to remember. I tried to hide it from my family. I couldn't always.

But my brother was there without Mom or the doctor, so I could ask questions. "Tell me about the accident."

Shane shrugged then dropped into the chair beside my hospital bed. "Not much to tell. We were in a Jeep. Ran a red light and got T-boned. You were in the back with Aspen." He ran his hands over his face, but his eyes took on that crazy look he got when he was at a loss and couldn't control what was happening. "You're lucky you weren't killed and that the kid survived."

"What kid?"

Shane's eyes got wide, and he opened and closed mouth. "Ah, the one who hit us."

I stared at my brother hard, trying to figure out what he wasn't telling me. The debilitating pain returned with a vengeance as I tried to remember when we got hit.

"You should see how shitty you look."

I went with the subject change, not because I didn't want the answers but because it hurt too damn much. Maybe, as the doc said, my memories would return on their own. But as each day passed, I was losing hope.

A flash of light went off, and I blinked Shane back into focus. "What the hell, man?" Then he turned his phone around, and I got the first glimpse of how fucked up I was. The painkillers I'd been on after waking had made things fuzzy, and I hadn't bothered to look at myself in the bathroom mirror. Besides, I could barely go in there without help. It was goddammed embarrassing.

I took his phone from him, studying how swollen my face was. I didn't look like myself. "What the fuck?" It was freaking me out.

"The meds and the holes they had to drill in your fat fucking head to relieve the swelling in your brain are why you look like hell."

"Thanks for that." I handed his phone back. "Is all that going to impact football?" I lived for football. I loved my family, but the game gave me purpose, and I knew I wouldn't be okay without it.

He shrugged. "It shouldn't. You just need to work on getting better." He blinked and looked away for a second.

Me being all fucked up and in the hospital was hard on everyone, and that didn't escape me. Part of me wanted to get out. The other was afraid of what I'd go home to. "I'm on the team. A starter?" I didn't even know that. It made me feel helpless.

"Yeah, McAffrey is back while you're out. No one is happy about it. Coach has me on D for the most part. And"—he grinned—"I love it."

"You're a beast. I can see why you're on D."

"I've broken the record already for the most QB sacks."

I laughed. "Good thing we're on the same team. I hope we get picked up in the draft by the same team. It would be too weird to go against you… or our cousins." I wanted us to stay together, like always. Being in the hospital was making me feel isolated, and I didn't like it.

"I can't even think about the NFL. If Grandad has his way, I won't be going." He looked tired, and I noticed the dark circles under his eyes. "He's been working me to death. He thinks I need to start stepping up and fix things at the properties or make deliveries to the teams doing renovations every minute I'm not in class or practicing. Other gofer stuff too." He held my gaze. "Stay in the hospital as long as you can."

We talked for another half hour, but when he got a text, he said he had to go, and I was as alone as anyone could be in a hospital. What Shane had said about Grandad felt like an answer I'd been searching for, but I couldn't figure out why.

Not only that, but his griping didn't make sense. Grandad bent over backward to help us while running a busy and profitable company. He encouraged us to follow our dreams and knew we wanted to go into the NFL. Maybe he and Shane had gotten into an argument. None of it made sense.

I needed my memory back. There were too many holes in what he'd told me about the accident, and the same went for our cousins, Cole and Damon. Everyone was guarded and obviously dancing around the truth. I knew they had to be hiding something huge. I was partly afraid they would tell me I had been driving, even though Shane said I was in the back with that hot chick, Aspen. Still, nobody would answer my questions, and it freaked me out.

One of the nurses came in, checked my vitals, then asked if I needed anything. I didn't, not that she could give me anything anyway. I'd only been out of my medically induced coma for a few days. Thinking about it blew my mind.

I strapped on the Velcro wrist weights that Shane had brought me. They were the lightest set we had. But I felt weak as hell—I'd been lying there for a month. I was set to begin physical therapy the next day, but I wanted to do something now.

I couldn't believe how huge my arms were. Everything was. Five years had brought a lot of changes. I wasn't a beast like Shane, but as a quarterback, I wasn't expected to bulk up to that extent. I would get back in shape. If nothing else, I needed to play. It motivated me.

There were too many things Shane, Cole, Damon, Mom, and the doctors wouldn't tell me when I asked. They kept saying I needed to be patient and let my mind heal, but fuck that. Exercise was the one thing I could control. I could get my strength back and leave that place. I wanted back in the game.

My phone rang as I finished my stupid light shoulder presses. I undid the Velcro and picked it up with shaking hands. Ridiculous. I had to get my body back to how it had been. I assumed I'd been in great shape before the accident

A glance at the screen told me it was that Aspen chick. I had a new phone because mine had been trashed in the accident, and Shane had only programmed in a few numbers—family and Aspen. He said he'd done it so I wouldn't have to deal with punt bunnies and randos who might have had my number. The phone continued to ring. Mom had said Aspen and I were friends, so I answered. Whether or not we were friends, she was hot.

"Hey, Aspen." I hit the arrow on the bulky controller connected to my bed to turn down the TV. "Where've you been?"

"Hi. Um, just school and work. How are you feeling?"

"I'm fine." As if I would complain to a hot girl. Nope, that would only make me look weak, and I didn't need any more of that. "Why haven't you come back to see me? It's boring as hell here. I spend most of the daytime being poked and prodded, but I'm mostly by myself at night." Besides, I thought she might tell me the truth about what happened in the accident, because there sure as hell was something no one else would tell me.

"I wasn't sure you wanted me there. But I'll try to come in tomorrow since I'm not working the dinner shift."

"Why wouldn't I want you around, surfer girl?" There was silence for a few seconds. "Did I say something wrong?"

"No, I… why did you call me that? Do you remember me?"

"Shit, I'm sorry. Of all the things to remember about the past five years, I would want to remember you. You just… I don't know. You remind me of surfing. A pink bikini comes to mind, and to be honest, I wouldn't mind seeing you in it."

She laughed, and the sound was like sunshine. "Okay, yeah. Surfing's my thing, but what you just called me… it's a nickname you used for me before."

Before the accident fucked up my head. She seemed sad that I didn't remember her, and that was the last thing I wanted. There was something about this chick. I liked her—a lot. "I overheard the nurses today. They didn't know I was standing near the door and weren't aware that I could hear them." This was hard. I hadn't told anyone. "They mentioned my dad. I guess he was here."

"Are you okay with that? Did you see him?"

"Hell no. I would have had him kicked out if he tried to come in. I've never seen him in person before. Only on TV."

"Do you think he's trying to make up for… things?"

The way she said that was weird. *Seriously? My dad?* I wanted nothing to do with him, which was what he wanted from us. "He abandoned my mom when she was pregnant with us. Left her the house and figured that was good enough. He never gave her child support or tried to see us."

"I'm sorry. I didn't realize it was that bad."

"The thing is, I'm good with it. It's a life lesson, ya know? How not to treat my kid. If I have one, I'm going to stay, no matter what. That kid will always know how much I care."

"That's very admirable." Her voice broke a little.

"Are you okay?" I didn't understand why what I'd said affected her so much. The last thing I wanted to do was upset her. I hated it when anyone I loved cried. Like Mom… it was the worst, and I would do anything to make her happy. Never letting my dad into my life was one way.

"No, really. I'm fine. But don't you think your mom would want you to forgive your dad? Maybe hear him out?"

I snorted. She might sometimes act like she was open to it, but my mom was too good for that asshole. She didn't need him, and she didn't want him fucking up our lives for whatever selfish reason he might have had. "He hurt her. Abandoned her when she needed him most. It was a good thing Grandad helped when she needed it… not like her sister. Mainly because Aunt Linda has her own problems." I realized I probably wasn't making sense but kept going anyway. "Honestly, I can't even imagine how hellish it was for mom after Nona died. Grandad was no picnic then. He was lost in grief and got a little too involved in Mom's life, which we suspect was from fear. He'd already lost so much. He meant well, but he and Mom went head-to-head when he tried to get her to reduce her hours. He offered to take over more bills. That wasn't what Mom wanted, though."

"Does Shane feel the same way about your dad or how your grandad tries to get involved?"

That was a tricky question because I wasn't always sure. He used to, regarding our dad, or I thought he did. "Maybe? He should. But Shane's got a softer heart. He's quicker to forgive. It's something I worry about." The more I thought about it, my head throbbed. There was a memory in there somewhere, hammering to come out. I wished like crazy that it would, but I could do without the pain.

"I wasn't sure if I should've called, and I didn't mean to get so personal with all those questions. I just wanted to know how you're feeling."

"I'm fine. Just frustrated. The doctors aren't saying much. Only that I need to be patient and not try to force the memories. But it's weird to feel like I'm fourteen but not look like it." I chuckled in a half-assed way.

"I can't imagine. It's weird for me too."

Right there. "There's something between us, isn't there? Are you my girlfriend?"

She laughed but didn't answer me.

"It would be pretty great if you were." I wasn't lying about that. The girl was incredible looking, a freaking wet dream. "I can't stop thinking about you. And if you are my girlfriend, you should definitely come over. I don't remember losing my virginity, but we can pretend I'm losing it all over again." I wanted that right fucking now.

"I can tell you for sure that you're not a virgin."

"Want to help out with that? You can make me remember everything buried in my mind."

"I-I've got to go. I'll talk to you later, Phoenix."

She hung up, and I couldn't help but feel like I'd fucked up. It bothered me—a lot. I set my phone on the side table and lay back in bed. All I could think of was what it would be like to be with Aspen. My eyelids drifted shut, and those thoughts played on in my dreams.

CHAPTER FOUR

ASPEN

Sleep did not happen last night. All I could think of was what Phoenix had talked about and how he'd asked if I was his girlfriend. *What could I say?* "Sort of. We're fake dating" wouldn't go over without explanation, and I wasn't comfortable giving one.

Max emerged from the stairwell, and I caught up with him halfway down the hallway. I was so glad we were still friends, and I was really trying to be better about asking him about his life and not just focusing on mine. We were both done with classes for the day, and I wasn't scheduled to waitress that night at Dillon's, the off-campus diner.

"Thanks for going with me to my doctor's appointment."

He wrapped an arm around me and pulled me into his side. "You know I'm here for it, baby girl."

We exited the dorm and walked to the parking lot where I'd parked my car. Several girls looked our way. I didn't blame them. Max was good-looking in that sexy, mischievous way that actor James Marsden from the movie *27 Dresses* had. But Max was interested in guys.

"Are you sure you're okay to drive?" Max squeezed me.

"Yeah, weirdly enough, I am. I was unconscious, so the crash didn't affect me." Even though what I'd said was true, revisiting the thought of the accident wasn't what I wanted. I changed the subject to something much more fun. "What's going on with your dating life?" I still felt terrible for crashing his rebound romance a little over a month before. But the guy he'd had in his room was a tool. I'd done him a favor, and when Max and I had both apologized, he'd admitted as much.

"Jaxon from art class asked me out."

"Oh, nice!" Jaxon was a huge dude, and it was weird to see him with a sketchbook, his big hands dwarfing his drawing pencils. I pictured him playing basketball due to his height. "He's cute. Did you go out yet?"

"Nope." Max grinned and gave me another squeeze before letting go to get into the passenger side of my beater car. "We're going to Dillon's for dinner and then a movie."

"Fancy." I drew out the word as I got the car started, breathing a sigh of relief and sending a quick thanks to the car gods when the engine rumbled to life without stalling. It'd been doing that lately, and I did not want to dip into the baby fund to fix my rusty bucket-of-bolts hand-me-down car.

I still wasn't touching Phoenix's fight money. That was for the baby. And I suspected I would need it, especially if he didn't get his memory back.

Away from school, I let loose everything that swirled around in my mind and kept me up for hours. "I talked to Phoenix on the phone last night."

"Any progress?" Max put his phone away and gave me his full attention as we moved through the intersection.

"No. Not really. But he called me Surfer Girl. I about peed my pants."

"That is promising." Max tugged on a clump of my hair. "Some part of him knows who you are, even if his mind isn't ready to release the memories yet."

"That has to be it. It's giving me hope, at least. But holy shit. He told me he didn't remember losing his virginity."

"Phoenix Bennett, a virgin? The smoke-show, one-and-done hottie? We are talking about the same guy, right?"

"Okay, smart-ass." I laughed because it was funny if I didn't focus on the tragic parts. "He propositioned me to come over and take care of that for him."

"No, he didn't." Max burst out laughing. "How did you not run over there?"

He wasn't kidding. I had barely stopped myself. The things that boy could do… but that was the problem. Mentally, he was fourteen, not the college freshman I'd had mind-blowing sex with at the cove over the summer. "I keep thinking he'll remember and feel like I took advantage of him."

"Says no guy ever."

I pulled into the doctor's office parking lot and got out and went inside. After checking in and taking a seat in the waiting room, I confided the other thing that was bothering me. "He's more open than before the accident. He's not constantly defensive. We talked. That rarely happened without one of us blowing things out of proportion and storming off, mad."

"Then this could be an opportunity for you," Max said as the nurse called me back. "Do you want me to stay here?"

"No." I scrunched my nose. "I asked you to come with me for support, not wait out here." We followed the nurse, and I leaned close to him. "What did you mean about it being an opportunity?"

"To get to know him without his defensive shields."

The nurse took my blood pressure in the room and asked a few questions before saying the doctor would be in shortly.

I sat on the exam table, thankful to be wearing my street clothes instead of a hospital gown. It was just a checkup. I didn't expect much—or I hoped not much, considering the scare the baby had given me a few weeks back. "That's something I've thought of too. The giant chip on his shoulder isn't as big."

"Remember"—Max's voice was soft, and he held my gaze with a seriousness that had me leaning forward—"he shielded you. There's more to him than you saw before the accident. Maybe a friendship would develop if you opened up to him a little."

That surprised me a little, coming from Max, and I knew he was right. "Okay, I'll give it a shot."

A knock sounded at the door, and we both quieted as the doctor walked in. I made introductions. She went through a series of questions, making sure I was eating, drinking, and not experiencing any lasting trauma from the accident.

"You haven't gained any weight yet, and you're very small. Much smaller than I would expect. I think we should do an ultrasound and check on the baby."

Max and I exchanged looks, and then he extended his hand to take mine. I grasped it like the lifeline it was. Ever since the amniocentesis and then the accident, my doctor had been overly cautious. I was glad about that, but it also brought about a lot of fear, and that wasn't good for the baby or me.

The nurse rolled in the ultrasound machine and squeezed warm goo onto my slightly rounded stomach. A baby soccer ball pushed tightly against my skin. Max moved his chair closer as the doc made her usual measurements. Then she turned up the volume, and we got to listen to the fast staccato of my baby's heartbeat. Max and I exchanged grins. I loved that sound. It meant she was doing well and filled me with joy.

After a few more minutes, Dr. Fielding turned the screen toward us and went through everything. The baby was doing well, and she had no concerns. I was just small.

"Do you want to know the baby's sex?"

My heart skipped a beat. I already knew, but getting the validation was too much to pass up. "Yes."

She moved the wand on my stomach and stopped where the baby was flashing us. Both Max and I laughed. "Phoenix would have gotten a good laugh too." I missed him, and tears gathered in my eyes, but I blinked them away. Max gave me a sad smile.

"She's not shy," Dr. Fielding joked.

There wasn't much left to the appointment. I promised I was eating and taking my vitamins. It wasn't long until Max and I were at the reception desk, where I made my next appointment before we headed back to my car and toward campus.

It was the beginning of November and chilly for California but warm enough that I only needed a thin long-sleeved shirt and leggings. Max grabbed my hand, and we walked into the dorm together.

"Do you think I should tell Phoenix?"

"Tell him what?" Max paused at my door. "About how you're having a little girl? Or that the baby is his?"

"Just the little girl part."

He tucked my hair behind my ear. "I do. He'll eventually get his memory back. Don't listen to the pessimistic diagnosis from the doctors. He called you Surfer Girl. He'll come back. But if you withhold things other than the baby being his, it won't sit right with him."

"That's a good point." I played with my keys for a moment. "I'm going to go there and maybe talk to his mom about what I'm doing. She works nights, so I'll wait and call her after her shift. That's when she's in to see Phoenix, anyway."

"Good plan. Now, wish me luck!"

I rolled my eyes. "You don't need it. Jaxon is lucky to go out with you. And Max"—I paused with my hand on the door—"thanks for going with me."

"Aww." He hugged me. "I'll always go with you."

Back in my room and with Max on the way to his, one floor up, I dropped my keys on my desk and palmed my phone. I stretched out on my side on the narrow dorm bed, found

Phoenix's name, and hit the call button. It rang a few times before he answered.

"Hi."

"Hey, Aspen."

"How are you feeling?" It was the same question I started all our conversations with. But I was scared for him, and I did want to know his progress.

"I'm doing okay. Had physical therapy and managed to walk the length of the room and back without help."

He sounded so pissy. I couldn't imagine how frustrated he was. The guy was a top-tier athlete, so the whole process had to be difficult for him. I needed a minute. I couldn't speak without him knowing I was crying.

"John, the physical therapist, said I'm weeks ahead of where I should be. It's not good enough, though. Mom said the guy's great, but I need to be doing better. It's bad enough that I'm out for the football season, but I have to get back and be hella stronger next year."

"You will. I know it." I cleared my throat. "And it's a big deal, the walking across the room part. Don't downplay it. After the accident, we didn't know if you would survive. I've never been so scared in my life."

"Come over, Aspen," he coaxed, his deep voice intense. "Help me celebrate."

I was surprised by how much I wanted to. "I've got a paper due tomorrow, and I haven't started on it yet."

"It's lonely here. I could use the company. Please, Aspen. Bring your homework. I don't care if you have to spend some time working on it."

I shouldn't let his words sway me, and I knew it. "Okay, I'm leaving now." I wanted to see him too. *God help me.*

CHAPTER FIVE

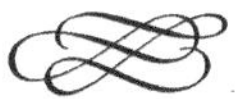

PHOENIX

Just thinking about Aspen made me hard. I had a few hot nurses, but they didn't do it for me. Ever since we talked about losing my virginity, fucking her was all I could think about. My body was ready whenever she entered my thoughts or we were in the same room.

I barely stopped myself from groaning. The bed was inclined so I could sit up, and my sheet was bunched around my waist, which was a good thing because knowing she would be there soon had made me rock hard. I would have given almost anything to have her climb on top of me. I just wasn't ballsy enough to ask, and the last thing I wanted to do was scare her away.

And man, my body was fucking huge. Even my dick was way bigger than I remembered. If I had any privacy, I would have taken care of things. But I was directly across from the nurses' station, and the nurse on duty was a hard-on antidote.

Strawberries and vanilla drifted into my room before Aspen walked in. She smelled so good and was just as hot as I remembered. Then I saw her. So beautiful. A flash of her golden skin and a pink bikini filled my mind's eye. She was standing next to a rusty car with a pink-and-silver surfboard strapped on top.

Pain sliced through my head, and the image disappeared just as quickly as it'd come. I breathed through the residual pain and held out my hand. The smile I gave her was shaky but genuine.

There was something about her that was worth any amount of head trauma. I wanted to be near her. "Come here. I want a hug."

She blushed, and it was so goddammed cute. Then she was in my arms, and jolts of awareness zinged between us. Her body was so firm yet soft, and her scent invaded my senses like a drug I never wanted to quit.

Holding her was better than anything I'd ever experienced. Not that I could remember much, but that was how it felt. I released her when she pulled back, but not without reluctance. She sat in the chair next to me, and I wished she would climb onto the bed so we were touching, but at least I could see her.

I was going to try to get information my family was withholding. I wanted to start slowly so she would be more relaxed and maybe tell me what I needed to know.

"I know this is weird"—I laughed—"because it definitely is for me. Thinking I'm fourteen, remembering the championship game, and the next five years are just… gone. But I want to know what I'm like. Am I different?"

"Than now?" She pursed her lips. "I-I don't know you well enough to answer that."

"My mom said we were friends."

"Yeah, but new friends."

"Were we at a party at the cove together?"

She cleared her throat. "Yes."

"When was the party?"

She looked around nervously. "It was in July."

I backed off from the personal angle. "Did you watch me in a game?"

She grinned, and her sky-blue eyes sparkled. "You're incredible. I was never a football fan, but I'm a fan after watching you play."

"I want to get drafted by the NFL. I'm guessing nothing's changed there."

"I believe you could do it. It's… crazy watching you play. The fans are intense. I got to sit with Riley, Sky, and Cass, and they had these amazing seats because of Cole and Damon. My sister and her boyfriend came too. You've got a great group with your cousins and their girlfriends."

I'd met Riley and Skylar. Cole and Damon came as often as they could, and usually, so did the girls. They were cool. I was glad they were in our tight-knit group too. "You didn't mention Shane. Is he an asshole to you?" My brother could be a tool.

"Shane and I haven't spent time together. I've run into him here and there." She shrugged. "Something is going on with him, but I don't know what it is."

"Before the accident?"

"Yeah. You would grumble about it sometimes. Maybe you can get him to open up to you?"

"He did a little. Something about our grandad."

"Okay, maybe that's it."

She looked unconvinced, but I let it drop because my head started to pound again. And it was a reaction I took note of. Anything heading in a relationship direction or if someone brought up Grandad, and my head hurt. There was a reason, and I paid attention to what my body was telling me.

I wanted to push myself—and Aspen—a little more. "How did we meet?" Because when we got off the phone a little while ago, I could have sworn her reaction said we were more than friends.

"Oh." Her eyes widened.

I had my answer. We were more than friends. I grinned but held back as much as I could. I didn't want to scare her away. I needed to know the parts of my life that had been lost in some weird void.

"It's what I already told you. We met at the party at the cove in July."

There was more to it. She just didn't want to say. "So we messed around?" There was no way I wouldn't have tried if I'd encountered a hot girl like her.

She blushed.

I was even more convinced. "You're my girlfriend, aren't you? Otherwise, you wouldn't be coming around."

"Um." She sank her teeth into her bottom lip then released it.

If she answered yes, I wondered if I could convince her to mess around some. The urge to touch her was intense, but the brewing headache amped up another degree.

"No. I'm not, not really." She glanced at her phone. "I've gotta go. That paper…"

"Sure." I closed my eyes against the pain. I didn't believe her. Even if we weren't dating, we were something.

"I'm going to go, but I'll call tomorrow. I hope you feel better, and congratulations on how far you've come with PT. That's huge, Phoenix."

I murmured thanks before forcing my eyelids open as she bent over me to kiss me on the cheek. I wasn't having that. I turned at the last second, colliding my lips with hers. One hand went behind her head, and I held her in place as my mouth slanted over hers. When she gasped, I took advantage and deepened the kiss.

Everything about it was fantastic. The way she responded, tasted, and felt was familiar yet new. It was the best fucking kiss I'd ever had in my life.

I didn't want to, but the headache was brewing to the point that I knew it would be unmanageable. I released my hold on her, breaking the kiss and letting her put some space between us. "Stay." Aside from the pain, I wasn't ready for her to leave.

She shook her head then ran out, but not before I caught a flash of pain on her face. Another sign that we were more than she was letting on. With nothing left to do for it tonight, I pressed the call button for the nurse. When she came in, I asked for pain medication. I needed to pass out and rest to push myself even harder in the morning.

I was going to do some serious fantasizing, and it would be all about Aspen.

CHAPTER SIX

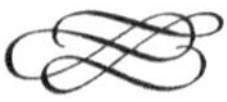

ASPEN

Holy crap, kissing Phoenix was a religious experience. On shaky legs, I rushed from his room to the connecting bridge that took me to the garage, then the elevator, and finally to my car. I felt a connection, a need to be with him the entire time. I wanted to turn around and accept his invitation to lie beside him and let him embrace me. But I couldn't.

He would find out about the baby. And even though I had been planning to tell him little things—not that I was pregnant with his kid but other stuff—I thought better of it. He was getting headaches, and I knew even though he didn't tell me. I didn't want to make things worse. He needed to heal and get out of the hospital.

I sat in my car, completely stalled, unable to leave or stay. The situation with Phoenix paralleled how I felt overall: suspended in time and with no real direction. Everything felt different, and he was different—not the physical challenges he faced because those were long and terrifying—but the kinder, less defensive side he showed me was new, and I liked it.

He didn't know the results of the amniocentesis. He'd missed out on pictures and ultrasounds, and I thought he would want to be a part of that. Deep down, even as annoyed as he'd made me with his attitude and lack of punctuality, I understood that he would be there for our baby. And that was all I had wanted.

Right?

Yes, that's it. My stance hadn't changed.

I wanted to give myself a chance to get to know him and to let him do the same with me, especially without the barriers we constantly threw up around each other before the accident. It wasn't lost on me that maybe we had a chance, since even with his memory of our time together gone, he still wanted me.

That kiss…

My skin heated as I remembered the way he'd controlled it. Mentally, he should have been behind, fumbling, not sure what to do with his tongue and teeth. But there had been none of that. The way his mouth consumed mine had been just as potent as before, maybe even more because I was falling so hard for him.

In that accident, he'd risked his life and shielded the baby and me, and I would never forget it. And for that reason alone, I was going to open up to him and show him who I was. In the process, I would learn everything I could about him. Maybe we would make it—not at a relationship, because I still didn't want to be anyone's girlfriend—but at being close friends who relied on one another.

Liar. You're lying to yourself.

I ignored my brain. I was standing firm in my thoughts on dating and marriage. Nothing would sway me.

But that kiss…

I drove to the dorms on autopilot. Everything was too much. I had to talk to someone. My go-to person was Max, but he was on a date, and I was not going to crash it. My sister, Regan, had texted earlier to tell me that she was with Dane's family at some Broadway production, and my friends Riley, Sky, and Cass were studying for an important exam. That left… Mom.

Riley, Sky, and Cass had gotten me a teal beanbag chair with a back and a matching ottoman. I loved it, and I planted myself there while I waited for Mom to answer.

"Aspen." Mom's voice had a smile to it. "I was just thinking about you. Your ears must be burning."

That was weird, but I didn't even care because it was comforting. I slouched in the chair, resting my head on the rounded beanbag back. "Mom, things are crazy, and I just… needed to talk."

"Well, I'm always here for you." Mom's smooth voice soothed me.

She hadn't always been there for me, but I would take it. "Are you and Dad still"—I refused to say "disappointed," which was their actual stance—"upset with me?"

She sighed, and I heard the scrape of a chair. I could almost see the kitchen chair moving against the tile floor.

"No, neither of us is upset with you. It was just a shock. And after everything we'd been through and the fights you and Regan have witnessed between us"—a briskness snapped through her words—"it stunned us that you were following the same path."

I shifted uncomfortably, sinking farther into the beanbag chair. "Mom—"

"Hear me out, honey. As I said, it was a surprise. And your dad, he wanted so much more for you girls. He's so afraid that you'll be unhappy like I was."

"Was?" My eyebrows rose.

"Yes. We've been working on things. Going to counseling. It's not that we didn't have a connection or didn't love each other." Her chair creaked, telling me which one she was sitting in. "We just each carry so much resentment and use it as a weapon. But we're trying."

"Is it easier without Regan and me there?"

"Don't take this the wrong way, because we love you girls

more than anything, but yes." Her nails drummed on the kitchen table. "There's no one else to worry about but us. And we've found that we can pause in moments and listen to each other. We've both tried to put ourselves in the other's shoes and hear why they said something or what the problem is without snap judgment and defensiveness."

"That's great, Mom. I'm happy for you guys."

"Thanks, honey. So long drawn-out explanation aside, we're not upset with you. We want what's best for you, whatever that may be."

"Mom, things are a mess. Phoenix still thinks he's fourteen. He doesn't know about the baby, and I feel like I'm lying to him and keeping things like the ultrasound from him. And I worry that when he gets his memory back—if he gets it back—he won't forgive me for not telling him."

"That boy will forgive you. I saw the way he looked at you when we met him. And Regan was gushing about him before her trip."

"But—"

"He's a little rough around the relationship edges? Honey, that's how a lot of men are. But how he took care of you by getting you away while Dad and I were fighting at the table that first time we met. He took control of the conversation and backed you up. And let's not leave out how he looked at you when you were preoccupied and didn't notice. That boy is very into you. He won't hold anything against you. This is an impossible situation, and I'm sure he knows that on some level."

"Maybe." I squeezed my eyes shut. "I'm just worried and frustrated."

"I can't even imagine what you're going through. Do you want to come home? Is there anything you need?"

"No. I'm fine. I promise."

"Just hang in there and try to stay calm. Stress isn't good for you or the baby."

"I will." I paused. "I love you, and please tell Dad the same." I didn't tell them that enough.

"We love you too. Call anytime you want to talk or if you need us."

"I will, thanks. And Mom, I'm really happy for you and Dad and that you're working things out. Thanks for telling me. I need to go, though. I have homework."

We disconnected, and I pulled my backpack over and got to work on math. I grabbed my phone and found my go-to homework classical playlist. Once the clear cadence of harmonic instruments crooned from my speaker, I scanned my homework. There were only about ten problems to complete. My pencil scratched over the paper as I worked on the problems, making sure to show my work. I liked math. It was analytical and enabled me to go through the steps without too much thought. Sometime later, someone knocked on the door.

I set my laptop on the floor and rolled out of the beanbag chair. I couldn't imagine what it would be like to heave myself out of that thing once my stomach was huge. I hoped it didn't get too big. Body changes sucked. I already had to pee ninety-five times a day, my boobs were getting weird, and I wasn't looking forward to the hemorrhoids I'd read about in *What to Expect When You're Expecting.*

When I opened the door, I almost cried in relief—crying was apparently another of my pregnancy things. Riley, Sky, and Cass stood there, and I couldn't have been happier to see them. I ushered them in, eyeing the drinks they carried from the coffee place. It was late, so I wasn't sure what was going on.

"I see that look on your face." Riley grinned. "Decaf, every single one of them."

"Including that chai tea thing you like." Sky passed me a cup.

"Yum. Thank you. My mood just got miraculously better."

"What's the problem? Phoenix being a drag?" Cass winked.

"Oh no… I so know that look. Phoenix and I go way back. No need to defend our QB. I'm only teasing."

"Emotions." I waved off what I knew was my resting bitch face. "And"—I looked to the ceiling, confused by my new reality—"I'm worried about him. Also, can I say that he is way more agreeable in his current mental state as a fourteen-year-old than he is at nineteen?"

Sky smirked as she fell onto my bed, tugging one of my throw pillows over and hugging it to her stomach. "It's because he sees you as part of his inner circle. If you were just some girl, he would be an asshat. I knew him at fourteen, so trust me. The guys were some stupid elite group that everyone bowed down to, even then."

"Because they're incredible athletes and hot as hell," Cass said, taking the desk chair and crossing her legs.

I tilted my head, not believing their decaf story given the amount of energy that trailed their restless movements.

"Don't let miss I-hate-all-athletes get in your head. The guys weren't all that bad."

Riley snorted as she settled on the bed next to Sky, her back against the wall. "They're assholes."

"Well"—Cass rolled her eyes—"you have every reason to think that. But things are different now. They've grown up a bit."

"They are. Cole and I had lots of run-ins, and he made things challenging for me, but that's all in the past. And… full disclosure, I gave him hell back and loved every second of it."

"Yeah, you really did." Cass high-fived Riley then moved from the chair to jump onto my bed. "We brought snacks, and we want to hear everything."

"What do you mean?" I got a little preoccupied with the food they brought. "About what?"

"The baby." Skylar elbowed her way off the bed and moved

to the floor next to me then placed her hand on my tiny soccer ball. "Have you felt it move yet?"

"It?" Riley's brows rose. "You know what the sex is, right? You're around four months, so…"

My lips twitched, and a rush of happiness filled me. "It's a girl."

"Holy shit!" Sky screeched. "This is the best news ever! There are too many boys and so much testosterone with Cole, Damon, Phoenix, and Shane. Don't get me wrong. I love them, but we need more girls to balance everything out."

Cass glared at Sky. "Um, why aren't you including Matt?"

"Matt's got that chill vibe like Aspen. He doesn't count."

"What do you mean?" I understood the chill-vibe thing—that had been my usual demeanor and outlook on life. Everything was low-stress when my parents weren't trying to kill each other verbally.

"You haven't met him yet, but he's a laid-back surfer and so, so gorgeous," Cass gushed. "And he's all mine."

I laughed at her lighthearted possessiveness. The nagging thoughts weren't far, though, and my friends must have seen them in my expression. Sky asked what was bothering me.

"I don't like keeping things from Phoenix, but I can't tell him I'm pregnant or that the baby is his. It's driving me crazy." I rambled. "He doesn't know that the amniocentesis results came back negative, he hasn't seen the latest ultrasound pictures, and he doesn't know we're having a little girl. Like… how can a guy who lost five years and has no memories past the age of fourteen be a dad?"

"Hey"—Riley moved to my side and wrapped an arm around me—"we're here for you. All of us, and that includes the guys. Phoenix will understand, and I know he'll come back to us. He just needs time to heal."

I got that, but convincing myself enough to stop stressing so much was another story entirely.

They stayed for an hour, sharing stories about the guys and how they handled them when they first started dating. They drew me into their world even more, and it felt fantastic. I liked them a lot, and we made plans to hang out over the weekend.

When they left, Phoenix was back on my mind. And so was that kiss. Before I could stop, I sent him a text saying that I hoped he felt better.

He texted back immediately, asking if he could video call me.

It wasn't a good idea, but I said yes then answered when the call came through.

His gorgeous face filled the screen. The swelling had gone down significantly, and he looked like every gorgeous, sexy inch of himself again. His silver eyes swirled, and I couldn't stop a grin from hijacking my mouth. "How's it going there? You're going home soon, right?"

"Not soon enough." His mouth formed a slash. ESPN droned on in the background. "Tomorrow, actually, but that just means another night of shitty sleep."

"I mean, you are right by the nurses' station." His mom loved his room's location, mainly because of the potential for extra attention and quick reactions, should they be needed. I wanted to ask if he felt weird about going home to recover more instead of back to school, but his mind still thought he was in high school. "Will it just be you and your mom when you go home?"

"Yeah. Shane has football, the fucker. I can't stand missing the rest of the season. Not that I remember playing in college, but it had to be incredible."

He looked so disgruntled I had to stifle a laugh. He wouldn't have appreciated it. I looked for something encouraging to say. "You were incredible, once your hand healed." I flinched, swearing under my breath.

He raised his hand and waved it in front of the screen. "This scar? Shane filled me in on some of the details. Not everything, I'm sure… but he's not as cagey with details as everyone else."

I bit my lower lip, swallowing anything negative before pasting on a neutral expression. "He's your twin. I would think that's expected."

Phoenix tilted his head, and silence filled the space between us. "Has he been a dick to you?"

"Shane?" Panic whipped through me. I didn't want to cause any stress. We needed a topic change, stat. "We barely talk. Not like I do with Riley, Sky, and Cass, anyway."

He laughed, letting the topic of his brother drop. "I remember Cass and Sky from high school. We didn't interact much then, but I'm guessing that's changed since Riley's with Cole. I know I like her. I can feel it." Frustration bracketed his mouth. "I just don't remember, which is getting old."

"Have you remembered anything more?" I shouldn't have asked, but the truth was that every time we talked, I struggled not to tell him anything about the baby.

"Not really." He raked a hand through his light hair. It was longer than before the accident, and my fingers itched to touch it. "There are some fuzzy images, but nothing I can grasp yet."

A nurse came in to take his vitals, and my eyelids drooped. I didn't want to get off the phone with him, but I laid my head on my arm, changing the angle of the screen, and relaxed into the mattress even more.

It wasn't until I yawned three times in a row that he told me how much he liked talking to me. And I thought he mentioned something about our kiss, but I couldn't keep my eyes open.

In my dreams, I could relive it many times over.

CHAPTER SEVEN

PHOENIX

"Ready to get out of here?" Shane strolled into my room with a shit-eating grin on his face. "I'm chauffeuring your ass home."

"About time." I finished another small lap of my room then leaned against the hospital bed that I never wanted to see again, especially after being there for just over a month. I didn't even care that he was forty-five minutes later than he said he would be when he called to tell me that he, and not Mom, was picking me up. I just wanted to leave the confinement of that place. I could only walk up and down the halls so many times. I hit the call button, and a few minutes later, one of the nurses came in.

"Ah." Michelle smiled. "Your ride's here. I'll get those papers for you, and the doctor also needs to sign off. Just give me a minute."

"Thanks." I sat back on the bed and tapped my foot against the tile floor. "Are you missing classes?"

Shane shrugged. "I emailed the professors. It's fine."

It meant something, him being there. "Thanks, man."

We talked about the latest game while we waited. The hospital release took much longer than it should have. Doctors had to sign off, and then there were instructions and having to make the physical therapy appointments. Shane revealed that Mom had called him in to spring me from the hospital after a five-car pileup derailed her release from her ER duties. Just the mention of the crash was enough to send chills cascading over my body, further fueling my need to get out of there.

"That was crazy." Shane straightened and moved to the side of the entrance, where several nurses waved before going back inside. His clipped responses echoed my impatience. He'd been in just as much of a hurry and pushed the process along as quickly as he could. Neither of us liked to be a patient in the hospital, and knowing my brother, it was killing him that it had been me in there. It would've for me if had been him.

We didn't need to express every thought and feeling between us because we could feel it—we were twins and were tethered together whether we liked it or not. I had an odd sense that I'd been reading something off about him for a while, even if I couldn't remember what. It was there in the way his eyes would stray away from mine, as if he could barely contain whatever was bothering him. But there was enough going on as it was, and eventually, he would tell me. Or I would make him.

Mindy, the charge nurse, winked as she accepted the papers I'd signed then took them back to wherever she needed them to go. My muscles were stiff, and I grunted as I stood then settled into the ridiculous wheelchair Mindy steered my way.

Everyone was cool, but the nurses flirting with me was a little off-putting, which was weird. Normally, I would have been into it, but I kept thinking about Aspen and only Aspen.

Shane snapped another picture, and I growled at him, silently plotting payback as he slipped from the room to pull the car around while Mindy wheeled me out. We waited for him to pull up, making small talk until he arrived. After thanking her, I got out and into Shane's car. Seat belt on, I turned toward him as he pulled away. "How did you break me out of there without Mom coming?"

Finally, we were in the car after that embarrassing wheel-chair ride, which my asshole brother documented with a video he put on social media and that picture, which he set as his screensaver.

"She's been working too hard and worrying just as much. The accident she had to work the double shift for must've been tough, and she'd just gotten home when I pulled up. After she talked to the doctor on the phone about your progress, she passed out on the couch. I carried her to her room and made sure it was dark. That's the only reason she wasn't there, and she won't be happy to find out you got out early without her."

"Nothing about this is great. I've got a lot of PT until I can go back to school, and I have no idea how I'll be able to handle the workload."

Shane took his eyes off the road for a moment. Guilt was painted all over his face, which was nearly identical to mine. Even if I hadn't been able to read his features like a book, I could feel it radiating off him. We were usually in perfect tune with each other as a routine part of our lives.

"You've got a tutor. Remember Noel Simon?"

"Oh, yeah." I grinned. She was cute and a total brainiac. "Wait. Why the hell aren't *you* helping me?" Maybe that was the guilt I was getting off him.

He winced. "Grandad has shit for me to do every day. And if I don't do it, or if I'm late…" He slammed his palm against the steering wheel multiple times. "I'm sick and tired of getting bitched at about it."

"What's his deal?" I wasn't following, but the mention of Grandad wasn't sitting right with me, and I had no idea why. "He knows you have school and football."

"Doesn't matter. He's on my ass. He wants me to know his business's ins and outs for when we take it over."

"Whoa, that's not in our plan. Or not mine, anyway. Did he have me doing that stuff too?" Finally, someone was talking to me like I wasn't fucked in the head. The constant tiptoeing around everyone was doing was pissing me off and making me even more determined to regain what I'd lost.

"No," Shane growled. "He seemed to have singled me out. I have no idea why. Maybe because he knows about Aspen? With Grandad, you never know. He's a sneaky bastard, something I'm coming to find out more and more."

"What are you talking about?"

"What?" Shane changed the station on the radio then turned it way up. "Grandad being sneaky," he shouted over some annoying song. "He is. What're you going to do at home? Can you get around at all?"

"Stop changing the subject." I turned the radio down.

Shane sped up, and we flew down the highway.

"What's there to know about Aspen?"

"Nothing. I'm just annoyed. At school, there's this little prick, Luke Green. I punched him the other day."

"On school property?"

"Yeah, I know." Shane clenched his jaw. "But Coach didn't find out about it, so I'm good."

"You're lucky. You could have gotten kicked off the team. What about the fights? Are those still happening?" We'd just started them—wait. We started them when I was fourteen.

"They are, and Jake Flynn wants a rematch with you."

I had no idea who Flynn was, but I wanted to get back in the ring. Our cousin Cole had started the underground league his first year in high school. We weren't long to follow, and it was the best way to get aggression out. I was glad I remembered. It'd been going on before our state championship game, so I wasn't surprised that I did, but still… it would've been nice if more memories followed. I needed my brain to make more progress so I could get my life back. "I'm in. I just need a little time to get my body working right."

"I don't know if it's a good idea. Do you remember him?"

"No, but does it matter?" I flashed him a cocky grin. All four of us were badasses in the ring. I wasn't worried.

"He's a huge guy. And…"

"Shut up. I didn't say right now. I'll be back to normal in a month."

"That's ambitious." Shane's frown deepened, and he shot me another look as he pulled into the driveway.

I had to live with Mom for a while before I was cleared to go back to school and the football house. It had been strange to realize I was living away from home. Everything was hard to understand because I felt like a freshman in high school, not college. "You know I can do it. A month is plenty of time to build my strength and endurance back to where it was." *Where's the faith?*

"Just don't do too much. We thought we were going to lose you." He started to get choked up, and I made a weak attempt to punch him in the shoulder. Neither of us commented on it.

"There's a lot I still don't know."

"There is, but don't stress about it. I know it'll come back. It has to."

I agreed. There was no way I would be left behind anywhere, but especially with football. I had made a D1 team, and Shane said I was starting quarterback. That was golden and moved me so much closer to my goals.

We pulled into the driveway, where I refused to let Shane help me. When he hopped out of his side, I got my door open and swung my legs down, using the door to brace myself. I had to stand there for a few seconds before I was sure my legs would hold me. That shit was so weird. I just wanted to be myself again.

Shane hovered, and I hated every second of it. I think he did too. I was more determined than ever to speed up the process and get my life back. Mom was asleep, which was fine with me. She had said I was staying in the downstairs guest room, but for the time being, I wanted familiarity. I would move when she woke. I was fucking exhausted. By the time I got to my room—first time with stairs since the accident—and Shane dumped my stuff there, I had enough energy to lie on the bed, and that was in. Within minutes, I was sawing logs.

When I woke, it wasn't nearly as bright out. I glanced at my phone for the time when a text came through from Aspen: *Went to the hospital to see you. Glad you got to go home.*

I'd planned to call her when I got home, but then I passed out like a fucking baby. Talking to her—or even better, being around her—was the best part of my days. And if I could lock down whatever was between us, I bet I could have her in my arms at night too. There were some intense vibes between us. I still hoped she was actually my girlfriend.

Me: *Sorry about that. Want to come over?*

Three dots appeared on the screen then disappeared. It happened a few more times, and I started to get annoyed.

Aspen: *Sure, but it'll be later. I have something to do first.*

I didn't like that. Not even a little. *Is she seeing some other guy since her boyfriend got all fucked up in the head and forgot everything about her?*

Aspen: *I have to have dinner with my family. I can come after that.*

Fuck yes. We would repeat that amazing kiss because I'd never wanted anything more.

CHAPTER EIGHT

ASPEN

The heavy silence in my parents' house unsettled me. It was nothing like what I'd grown up with. In the kitchen, they worked side-by-side to get the meal ready. They weren't talking, but the lack of arguing was as disturbing as it would have been if they were making out.

For the second time, I wondered if coming to dinner had been a smart move on my part. I set a bowl of mixed greens on the circular kitchen table that had seen better days and took my usual spot. Dad placed a pot roast in the center, and Mom carried in a small bowl of fruit. She'd always liked to add strawberries to her salad.

"So"—I spread my napkin in my lap—"how are things going?"

"Great." Mom's smile looked strained. "I talked to Regan. Things are going well with the portfolio she's working on for her fashion class next year."

Why haven't I heard about this? "What are you talking about?"

"Oh, I didn't realize you hadn't heard. Because she won that scholarship, she met with the director of the fashion department, and he proposed a lookbook, or something like that, with sketches she designed for the fall. It'll be a project that she and a few of the other honors students will work on. Then they'll collaborate for the fall fashion show the school plans to put on."

"Wow, that's exciting." I missed my sister like crazy. We were due for another long phone conversation. "I'm glad things are going so well. Do you miss having her home?"

"Of course." Mom's smile was sad, but she glanced at Dad, and her features softened. "But we're enjoying our time together."

The whole scene was so weird. It was like I'd entered the twilight zone. My parents fought. That was what they did. I wondered if they were still getting divorced but was almost afraid to ask. The lines between Dad's eyebrows lessened when Mom caught his gaze before he returned it to his food.

For a moment, things seemed almost good. But then he withdrew into himself again. Maybe he was trying not to scream at me like he had in the hospital. I still couldn't bring myself to fully forgive him for what he'd said. The sound of the tray and all the instruments clattering to the floor when he'd bumped into it screamed through my mind, followed by his horrific words: *You survived a potentially fatal car accident but emerged with your problem intact.*

"How's Phoenix doing?" Mom asked, effectively pulling me from the cringy memory.

"He's about the same." I dished some potatoes onto my plate before passing the bowl to Dad. "He still thinks he's fourteen."

Mom paused, the salad tongs suspended over her plate. "He still doesn't remember about the baby? About your relationship?"

My heart stuttered. It hurt that he didn't remember me, but in a way, things were so much better. "No. But it's not all bad. He wants me around all the time, which makes me think somewhere in his subconscious, he knows what we had and doesn't want to let it slip away." I shrugged. That was a lot to admit.

"What about his football career? Will he be able to play again?" Dad asked.

I almost dropped my fork. He'd refused to look at me when I came in and hadn't spoken to me in weeks. I was surprised he'd addressed me at all.

"He'll be fine. Physically, he's recovering, and from what I've heard, nothing will prevent him from returning to the game next year."

"Hmm." Dad flicked his gaze to me before returning it to the pot roast he was systematically demolishing. "What will happen to you and the baby when he gets an NFL offer? Or if he doesn't?"

"I'm capable of taking care of myself." My hand shook, probably with the effort it took to keep my voice calm. "I'm not without skills."

"Honey"—Mom's rested a hand on Dad's, but her words were for me—"that's not what your father meant. He's worried about how you'll support yourself and a baby. It's not easy to do it on your own."

"Well, it's a good thing I'm not, then." I shoved a large forkful of salad into my mouth and chewed angrily. They knew nothing about the business I was already working on setting up or how both versions of Phoenix had refused to abandon his child. Even if I had trouble making ends meet, I knew he would find a way to give our child what she needed.

No one said anything for several minutes, and I stewed silently. Mom had defended Dad. It was… weird. I wished my sister had been there to witness it—she wouldn't believe it when I told her.

"How's work at the diner?" Mom's voice was slightly high-pitched.

I let the moment go, following her lead with a subject change. "It's great. I like Dillon, the owner, a lot. He's also super flexible with our shifts, and the other girls are fun to work with."

"Aren't you exhausted?" Mom pushed her mashed potatoes around on her plate while Dad heaped more pot roast onto his. "I remember when I was pregnant with you, I needed to take so many naps."

I shrugged, warding off the arctic blast her comment seemed to stir from Dad. "I'm tired, but I find time for a power nap here and there. It's been okay, and I like getting out and working."

Dad shook his head. "Of the two of you girls, I never thought it would be you."

"Honey." Mom squeezed his hand before turning to me. "What about friends?"

I ignored Dad and continued to answer her. "Max is my closest friend. I think I told you about him. We met in 2D art class at the beginning of the semester."

"Oh, yes. Very handsome."

I smiled. "Yep, he is." It was clear she hadn't picked up on how platonic our relationship was. Phoenix might have been someone my dad would have liked before he found out about the baby, but Mom was a tougher sell when it came to settling on one person. "I also go to the beach with a few girls."

"Other surfers?"

"Two of the girls surf, and one doesn't. You might have heard of Riley Matthews." Dad read those alumni magazines religiously. He had to have heard of her.

"The Olympic hopeful?" His face revealed nothing.

What is going on with him? It's like he can barely stand to be at the same table as me. "Yeah, she's pretty cool and is also dating Cole Savage."

"Phoenix's cousin, right?" Mom looked to Dad for confirmation.

He nodded then stood and took his plate to the sink, turning his back on us. I glanced at Mom, catching her as she closed her eyes for a brief respite. They were more of a united front than ever before. I could tell in the moment when she defended him. Still, I was pissed.

"Why did you want me to come when you don't even talk to me?" I stood. I was over it. Mom might have been acting cool, but Dad was not. "I'm going." I was enraged by how he was behaving, but behind the anger was deep sadness. I would deal with that later. "You're being judgmental, and your unhappiness with whatever—me, life, I don't know—is toxic. And I gotta go."

"Aspen." Mom jumped up from the table and followed me. Of course, Dad hadn't moved. "I'm so sorry. Something happened at work today, and he's processing."

"It's whatever. I'll talk to you later." I hugged her then left. I couldn't get out of there quickly enough.

It took three tries to start my car. As soon as the engine turned over and held, I headed home. *What am I going to do?* My ancient car needed work, which cost money. Phoenix wanted me to come over, and I badly wanted to go. I genuinely liked talking to him. It wasn't like before. There was patience and understanding there. He asked me questions about my day, family, and surfing. And he listened, genuinely interested in my answers. I felt like he really saw me. That part of our relationship had been severely lacking prior to the accident.

And when he regained his memories, I hoped he would remember New Phoenix and not regress. The guy had been an alpha asshole. I still got glimpses of that at times, but it wasn't enough to raise my defenses, and he usually got it under control pretty quickly.

Cass had said he viewed me as part of his inner circle. I wanted to stay there and bask in the sunlight. Before the accident, I'd been on the outside. But the girls spilling so much about the guys and their history with them made me understand it more. The guys were intensely protective, and their sheer possessiveness was unparalleled with people they loved and trusted. I wanted to maintain a hold of that with Phoenix if, by some miracle, he didn't shove me away when he remembered he was nineteen and the reasons why he'd perceived me as he had.

I wasn't far from where Phoenix lived, but I wasn't sure if I could keep my eyes open when I was there. I pulled over and called him.

"Are you on your way?"

I shivered from the effect of his deep voice. It brought images of sex and dominance. Why I liked that about him was a mystery. Okay, it wasn't. He was incredible, and what he'd done to my body—I wanted more of that again.

"I think I'm going to go back to the dorms. I'm exhausted."

"You can rest here. It's not like I can do a lot. And I miss you."

Oh, wow. Phoenix Bennett misses me? I wanted to call Max and tell him about the momentous turn of events. And I would tell my best friend, but later. After Phoenix saying that to me, there was no way I couldn't go to his place. "Okay. I'll be there in ten minutes. I can't stay long, though, not with the drive back to school and how tired I am."

When I pulled into his driveway, the front door opened, and Phoenix stood there in the fading light. I gave him a small wave. Before I twisted the keys, the engine made an unsettling sputtering noise then died. *Fuck my life.* I dropped my head to the steering wheel and got control of my panicked emotions before leaving the car with a smile that I didn't feel.

He looked so good that my mood flipped from bad to good, the problems with my car and Dad fading immediately. "Are you pushing your recovery?" It fit his personality to do that.

He shrugged.

"Yes, he is!" His mom appeared behind him, dressed in scrubs. Her dark-brown, almost-black hair was pulled into a low ponytail, which only accentuated her beauty. "Hi, Aspen. I'm so glad you're here. Come in."

"Hi, Mrs. Bennett."

"Ugh." She scrunched her nose, blue eyes sparkling as she waved me in. "Call me Cece." She winked. "We've already been over that."

I smiled, pushing my nerves aside. "Sorry. I'll remember in the future."

Phoenix shot a worried glance at my car then stepped to the side.

"Thanks for having me."

The three of us went inside, and Cece hugged me before she got ready to leave for work.

"There's a second spare bedroom all made up on the first floor, facing the front. Phoenix is in the one off the kitchen. Please feel free to stay the night. I would feel better if you did. Shane can't be here because of some school stuff and practice, I think, and I hate leaving Phoenix alone."

"Mom"—he leaned against the wall—"I'm fine. But Aspen can stay. Just don't worry so much. I'm okay. Promise."

Tears gathered in her eyes, and she hugged her son. "I know you are, but I worry. Remember—both of you—call me if anything happens, no matter how insignificant you think it is."

We both promised, and Phoenix's cheeks turned adorably pink. He treated his mom so well. I loved seeing that side of him. When she left, he grabbed my hand, and his grip was surprisingly strong compared to the other day in the hospital. "Let's go out by the pool. You seem like you like being by the water."

"I do, but why do you say that?" The slider was already open, and we went to a patio that surrounded a stunning pool with the beach as the backdrop just past the wrought iron gates. "Wow. This place is…"

"We like it. It's a lot for Mom to keep up with without Shane and me at home. There's so much I want to do for her. I just need to get into the NFL, and then she won't ever have to work another day in her life."

My heart swelled, and I missed my footing.

Phoenix helped steady me then laughed. "I'm the one who's unsteady on my feet. It's nice that I get to save someone else from face-planting for a change."

He held me tight, and in light of the shock that had me tripping from realizing how I felt about him, I let him. He sat on a lounge chair and guided me to sit between his legs. It wasn't a good idea. He might feel the baby. I shook my head, offered a weak smile, then took the chair next to him.

I was stunned by how much I cared about him. It was all those late-night conversations and how he treated me like I was the only one he saw, even in spite of the younger nurses doing their best flirting routines. He never paid attention to their antics or encouraged them.

Curled on my side, I had one hand under my cheek to look at him, keeping the pool still in partial view. Before I could stop myself, I yawned. "I'm sorry. I'm tired. It's been a long day."

"You can sleep if you want. I'm happy you're here whether you're awake or not. We can talk after you get some rest."

It was warm outside, even though it was getting close to Thanksgiving. "We'll be on break from school soon. Are you going to be able to go back after?" It was probably too early, especially since his memories hadn't returned.

Phoenix hooked his hand under my chair and tugged it closer. He was getting his strength back. "The doctor thinks I should wait until next semester. I want to go back, but without football, it's not a bad idea to wait and get stronger before I do." He tucked a strand of my hair that had fallen to rest on my cheek behind my ear. "And since I can't drive yet, why don't you leave that piece of rust you drove here in the garage and take my SUV to school? You can use that to come back and forth, and I won't worry about your car breaking down halfway here."

"No way. I can't take your car." I curled my knees toward my chest. "Besides, that thing probably costs a fortune to fill up."

He shrugged. "My uncle bought SUVs for my brother, me, and our cousins, and a gas card came with it. He pays the bill. Just use that, and you won't have to worry about it. I'll let him know. He won't care."

"That's incredibly generous, but there's no way I can do that."

"You can. When Mom hugged me, she suggested it." He chuckled, the deep cadence of his laugh spreading warmth in its wake. "Not that I wasn't already thinking it when your car died in the driveway. And you don't have your keys, anyway. When you set your stuff down inside, she swiped them, so you don't have a choice."

"Wow, you guys are devious." Guilt ate at me. I needed to talk to her about the baby, even if I couldn't tell Phoenix. A part of me thought she already knew. She'd looked over my chart after the accident and learned I was pregnant. And with Phoenix's protective instincts during the crash... maybe she'd put two and two together. Either way, she'd never made me feel uncomfortable or unwelcome.

I would tell her the first chance I got. Maybe tomorrow morning when she was off her shift. "Thank you."

"You're welcome. And trust me"—his grin turned wolfish—"it's for my benefit too. You'll have to come see me more often."

I laughed. "True. How's PT going? You're so much stronger already."

"I added a pool workout." He notched his head toward the pool. "It's helped a ton. And being home, I can control my nutrition with higher amounts of protein and more of what I need to heal faster. Plus, without everyone watching me like crazy, I've added in some light weights. Nothing too strenuous, but it's been a game changer."

"Do you miss throwing the ball? The games?" I pushed

myself up so I was sitting and facing him. Otherwise, I was liable to fall asleep, and I wasn't ready for our time to end.

"Yeah, it's a part of me, and without it, I'm drifting."

"I get it. I had to give up cliff diving a few months ago. I'm lucky I can still surf. It keeps me sane."

His brows furrowed. "Why did you have to give it up?"

"It was for a medical condition. I'd rather not talk about it. Besides, I have my art, and that saves me like football probably does for you."

"You're an artist?"

"Yep." I grinned. "My sister, Regan, and I were going to open up a shop as close to the beach as we could, where I would sell custom surfboards and she would have a line of board shorts and bathing suits. Regan's a genius with fashion design. I'm super proud of her. My little sis is going places."

"That's cool. Can I see something you drew? Or do you only work with paint?"

"I do both. I have a sketch pad in my purse."

"I'll get it." He stood and went into the house before I could stop him.

I worried my bottom lip. He was the one recovering from brain trauma, and I should have gotten up, not him. But he'd already stood and gone inside. My limbs felt so heavy. It was relaxing out there, and I didn't even want to dream about what it would be like to wake up to this every morning.

When he came back out, he handed me my purse, and I pulled out my sketchbook and gave it to him to look through.

As he flipped through the pages, I studied him. His blond hair was longer. The accident had weakened him, but one would never know it by looking at his body. His muscles were as defined as before. It was the ease of his smile that had changed. I could probably count on one hand the number of times Phoenix had smiled in my presence after I'd told him about the baby.

"These are incredible, Aspen."

I glanced at the page he'd paused on, his eyes rapidly moving over the swirls on the surfboard's surface. They had to be familiar to him, and I held my breath. The questions would come. I knew it. *Why did I let him go through the sketches?* Those were his tattoos drawn on the board, combined with the things I loved to do, and then there was the date tucked into one of the tribal designs of when we were together at the cove… when our baby was conceived. A pair of baby shoes stood out clearly. I didn't know what to do. I didn't want to lie to him.

"Hey."

I jumped out of my skin when Shane came out of nowhere, his voice harsh and annoyed. I took in his dark, messy hair and how his blue eyes snapped with fire. The brothers were so similar, just not in coloring or bulk. Phoenix had more of a quarterback's build, and Shane was built like a beast. The artist in me had dissected their facial structures, which were very similar, many times. Those high cheekbones and strong jawlines looked like they could cut glass. Chiseled and stunning. I'd drawn Phoenix too many times to count and was glad he wasn't holding *that* sketchbook.

"What's up?" Phoenix raised his gaze from my book to take in the agitated stance of his brother. "Mom said you wouldn't be home tonight."

"Yeah, well, things change. Grandad's here to see you."

I took my sketchbook back from him and stuffed it into my crossbody bag. Phoenix took my hand when I stood, and I went into the house with him.

A tall man that vaguely resembled Shane in coloring stood by the kitchen island, placing a white bag on the counter that smelled like fried chicken or something equally good. I smiled, but that died quickly when his faded blue eyes shot daggers in my direction. I'd never met the man in my life, but he seemed already to know about me and made an unfavorable judgment.

"Hi, Grandad. I wasn't expecting you, but it's good to see you." Phoenix waved a hand toward me, his smile wide. "This is Aspen."

I automatically moved forward and extended my hand. He shook it but released me immediately. He seemed agitated.

That was my cue to leave. I turned to Phoenix. "I should get going."

"Please stay." He took a step toward me.

"Thanks, but I need to go." I evaded his outstretched hand. "I have a lot of homework, and there's the drive back…" I needed keys and a car. Either one would be fine—just something to make my escape. Luckily, Phoenix understood.

"I'll be back, Grandad." He shot Shane a confused look before walking with me toward the door that led to the garage. There was a side table with a bowl with a couple of sets of keys. He handed me one. "The card is in the glove box. Let me know when you get back to school."

"Of course." I hugged him very carefully so he wouldn't feel the small round bulge.

Then I escaped, reminding myself that he had no memory of me or the last five years. *I've got to keep how I feel about him separate from who he was and who he is now.*

CHAPTER NINE

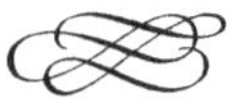

PHOENIX

Even though I hated being a human pincushion during acupuncture sessions, I did whatever the docs thought was best. They were my key to recovery, and I was determined to reach my end goal much earlier than expected.

After acupuncture, I downed water and a protein shake then went to physio and the sadist who headed up that department.

"Hi, Sarah."

"Phoenix." She didn't bother turning from the notes she was making on the computer.

Instead, I talked to her back, marveling how her short dirty-blond ponytail remained intact. She must have run her fingers through her hair before remembering she'd worn it up. She did that on occasion. The band was barely holding her thick hair in place. "Did you talk to the doc?"

She didn't answer immediately, so I got comfortable on her torture bed. It was just a massage table, but the deep tissue manipulation and stretches she put me through could be excruciating.

I wanted to get PRP injections—platelet rich plasma—and had brought it up to the neurologist and the rest of the team of doctors and physical therapists. The time I'd spent in the induced coma had done what they'd intended and reduced the swelling around my brain, but I wanted a faster and better recovery, and that meant PRP injections in addition to all the PT I was doing. I knew it would work. It was often used with elite athletes as an advanced treatment to assist recovery.

As a college student, it wasn't an option. Or maybe it was this hospital that didn't incorporate the practice. Whatever the case was, I hadn't been given the shots.

Sarah finished whatever she was doing on the computer and swiveled on her stool until we faced one another. "I got another no. I'm sorry, Phoenix, but it's not looking like it'll be an option. They don't feel you need it with how well you're doing, and it's a considerable expense."

I clenched my jaw, tired of hitting that wall. She motioned for me to stand. We went through her usual checklist, checking joint integrity and mobilization, motor control, function, postural stability, gait, sensory awareness, cognitive functioning, and perception.

Today wasn't a day for deep tissue manipulation, for which I was grateful. Sarah had the hand strength of a defensive guard. By the time I was on the treadmill, hooked up to electrodes she could monitor, my mind wandered. The docs thought my brain was in a good place. I disagreed. If it had been, I wouldn't have had all those voids where memories should have been or the incessant headaches. The neurologist assured me it was part of the healing process. I wanted to call bullshit but knew I needed to trust my docs.

My muscles flexed and bunched, and the miles faded under my feet. I lengthened my stride, pleased with how my body felt. I still couldn't drive myself to the sessions, but Mom, Shane, or one of my cousins took me a few times a week. Coach had finally agreed to download film to a tablet and sent it to me through Cole. The last thing I wanted was to return without being up-to-date on how the team played in my absence.

It was another hour before I finished and was released to return home. Exhaustion showed in the deep circles under Mom's eyes when she picked me up after her shift. I made my appointments as early as possible to accommodate her schedule, getting a ride from Raelyn when Mom was still working.

I was similarly beat, and we rode home in silence. After a few words and a hug, she went to her room and no doubt fell into a comatose state—she could barely keep her eyes open. My body was tired but in a good way. The PT and physio sessions weren't as strenuous as they'd been at the onset. I assumed I was stronger, closer to what I'd been before the accident.

With a large glass of water, I got situated on the couch and pulled the tablet over. As I watched the games, I made notes on what I saw that could be improved, partly for me, but I also sent them to Coach. I craved being a part of the team, and this kept me in the loop. It didn't hurt for him to know how serious I was about coming back. I was lucky my scholarship hadn't been revoked, and I knew I had him to thank for that.

Going back to the hospital for PT and the rest was weird. They pushed me, but I knew I was capable of more. That was where pool workouts came into play. After I got through a couple of hours of watching what Coach sent, I would log an hour in the pool.

I forced myself to down the water and then lost time going over film. Nothing would stop me from achieving my goals.

"Where's Shane?" Damon fell onto a chair by the pool, where I'd been spending most of my time since I got home a few days back.

Cole set a couple of pizza boxes on the table between us

before passing me a water. My cousins stopped by more often than my brother did. But Shane was still the only one who told me stuff, even unintentionally. Not everything but more than the rest.

I took a swig. "I don't know. Grandad has been driving him crazy. My guess is some bullshit errand for the company." Grandad and Shane hadn't stayed long the other day after Aspen left, and they'd acted weird the whole time.

"Huh. That's the first I've heard about Shane working for him. What's going on there?" Cole asked. "Is he interested in running the business? And I'm asking because we all know you're not."

I snorted then grabbed a slice of sausage pizza. "Not even a little. As for Shane…" I shrugged. "I don't know. He hasn't been home long enough for me to ask him."

"Well, he's a beast at practice, so I doubt he's given up on football." Damon stuffed half a piece in his mouth.

I hoovered mine as well. I was physically exhausted and hungry. I'd done a lot that day, starting with a long PT session that Mom had taken me to. When I got home, I had a protein shake then did a long workout in the pool. It felt amazing, but I had so far to go. I wanted to be there now—back at practice, starting in the games, and closer to Aspen.

"Is it weird?" Damon took another slice, his blue eyes boring into me.

"Is what weird?" I wasn't following.

"Thinking you're fourteen but looking like you do. Losing five years."

"It's fucking bizarre." I set my plate down and leaned back in my chair, enjoying the cool breeze coming off the ocean. "To know that I've finished four years of high school when I feel like I should be in class all day is a trip. Then I see you guys and Shane, and you're huge." I looked down at myself. "I am too. It's a lot to wrap my head around."

"It's weird for us too." Cole chugged half of his water. "And it's not the same on the field since you've been gone. McAffrey is back in."

The name sounded familiar, but my head started to throb, so I let it go.

"Dude"—Damon shook his head—"he threw an interception that cost us the game last weekend. And the guy cannot call an audible to save his life."

My gut tightened. "I want back in like you wouldn't believe." Cole understood. Out of all of us, he was as driven as I was.

"You've got to get better first," he replied calmly. "You'll come back stronger than ever, but don't rush it. This is your life, your future, and you need to give yourself time to heal." He pointed at me. "Don't fuck it up by rushing and pushing everything back even further."

"Yeah, I get that. It just sucks." I knocked his hand away. We needed a change of subject. "Shane told me Jake Flynn wants a rematch."

Damon's brows raised. "You're not considering that, are you? The guy is a monster."

"Did I beat him before?"

"Well, yeah, but you were pissed, and he was your scapegoat. No one would have beaten you that day."

"Why was I mad?"

My cousins exchanged a quick look, and I knew before either of them spoke that their response would be censored. "Forget it," Damon said.

Cole shut the empty pizza box, set it aside, and opened the other one. "Do you remember anything yet?"

"I have dreams or see flashes, but I don't know what they mean or if they're actual memories. They're mostly of Aspen."

"Riley and Sky love her." Cole grinned. "She's already a part of the group. Don't fuck it up."

"Why would I? Aspen's cool. And hot." More than that. I

wanted her, and I wasn't afraid to admit that to myself. I was dealing with some crazy stuff, but even knowing that I could have a five-minute phone conversation with her at the end of the day made the struggle worthwhile. I wanted to be more than her friend, and it seemed like we were moving in that direction, especially given how she'd responded when I kissed her. And if Grandad hadn't shown up, I would have kissed her again.

"Yeah, she is. We like her too." Damon narrowed his eyes at me. "Don't let anyone get in your head about her. She's already one of us. Don't make us kick you out to keep her."

"The fuck?" I threw my crust at him. "And what are you talking about? Who would get in my head?"

"No one," Cole snapped, glaring at his brother. "He just means your temper got out of hand the night you fought Jake. You were pissed because you thought someone was hitting on Aspen, but Max isn't into girls. He's her friend."

"She *is* my girlfriend, then." I laughed. Fuck yeah. Aspen and I were going to have a talk and then mess around.

My cousins stayed for another hour before leaving for practice, and I took a nap on the couch. I wasn't up to hauling myself off the couch and into my temporary first-floor bedroom. After the workouts and food, there was no option but sleep. The TV remote was on the coffee table. I palmed it and shuffled through a few stations until I found ESPN. I listened to the talking heads dissect the latest games as my eyelids grew heavier. It wasn't long before I drifted off to sleep.

The doorbell woke me from a deep sleep. Confused and startled, I hurried to the door as quickly as I could, worried that whoever was out there would wake my mom, who slept during the day because she worked third shift.

I yanked open the door to find a tall brunette on the top step. She was gorgeous, and if I hadn't been so into Aspen, I had a feeling I would be all over her.

"Oh, God. Phoenix." She launched herself at me.

My arms automatically went around her. Then I pried her off me and put a foot of space between us. I had no idea who she was or what she wanted, and even though my fourteen-year-old brain thought it could be interested, I felt nothing when we embraced and took notice. "Who are you?"

She covered her mouth with a hand, and her brown eyes grew wide. "Jillian. You don't remember me?"

"Nah. My memories are all fucked up right now." I swung the door wider because I was tired of being bored and alone. "How do we know each other?"

"I'm your girlfriend."

She wasn't. I might not have had any memory of the past five years, but I would've felt some attraction if that were true, and there was… nothing. I said nothing. I wanted to see what this chick would spill, especially since everyone else was so tight-lipped.

"You look incredible." She rested a hand on my bicep.

I moved so her hand fell away and went into the kitchen for a glass of water, knowing she would follow. My immediate urge was to call Aspen and ask her who the hell Jillian was, and I noticed that too. I filled a glass and held it up. "Want some?"

"No, thanks." She raised her eyebrows looked around the space—dead giveaway that it was her first time inside my home. It might not have been concrete evidence, but I read it all over her face. "You know anything about Jake Flynn? Shane tells me he wants a rematch."

"Jake Flynn? You fought him the night you got in that wreck. It was that pregnant slut Aspen's fault."

My hand tightened around the glass. I said nothing. I needed to hear more and blinked through the sudden surge of pain in my head.

"She started a rumor that you knocked her up. But no way. I didn't believe it. You always wear a condom." She batted her hooded eyelids at me. "I should know," she purred.

"Aspen's pregnant?"

"So she says, but don't believe her." Jillian came around the island and put her hands on my chest, wiggling closer. "She's trying to trap you. You didn't believe her either. That night after you beat the hell out of Jake Flynn at the fight, you punched Aspen in the face because she wouldn't have an abortion."

She was lying, and I blocked her out. All I'd heard was that Aspen was pregnant. *I could be the father.*

CHAPTER TEN

ASPEN

I *need to talk to you.*

I stopped in the middle of the sidewalk about four doors down from Dillon's, ready to work the evening shift, confused by Phoenix's text.

NOW.

I didn't have time for a conversation, so I shot off a message that said I was going to work and would catch up with him later. I dropped my phone into my bag then went inside.

In the back room, I shoved my stuff into the little cubby assigned to me and chatted with Adel, another server just getting off shift. I put on an apron and got ready to work.

Back on the main floor, I leaned against the bar as Nina, one of the other girls I worked with, waited for her drink order. "Hi." I smiled as she popped her gum.

"Hey, Aspen." She gave me a quick wave then filled her tray with the bartender's drinks before balancing it and moving away.

She weaved through the tables as Dillon, the owner, motioned me to the other end of the bar. Concern pulled at his usually relaxed features, and he glanced at the ceiling before returning his gaze to me. He absently scratched his short beard.

I waited for whatever he was going to say. He looked a little off, which made me paranoid. *Please don't fire me.* I was on time and worked hard, and I was pretty sure I hadn't done anything wrong or offended any customers. "Is everything okay? I ran into Adel in the back as she was leaving, and she said to cover section three. Did you want me to do something else instead?"

"I was going to have Rose come in and talk to you, but she's out of town this week."

Rose, his wife, occasionally worked the hostess station.

"I just wanted"—he blew out a breath and looked at the ceiling again before settling on my baby bump—"to make sure you were doing okay. If you need to get off your feet or take reduced hours, we'll make that happen."

Oh, phew. I laughed, more in relief than anything else. "You had me worried there for a second. I'm fine, but I'll let you know if anything changes."

"Good. Good." He nodded toward section three. "You're good to take over Adel's section. Did she brief you on what's going on with them?"

"Yep." There were only three tables, and she'd closed out two of them. I just had to check in on the last one to see if they needed anything else. "Is that it?" I couldn't help but grin because he looked like he wanted to flee.

"Yeah, we're good. I'm going to get some paperwork done in the office."

"Have fun." I grabbed my order pad as two people came in and were seated in my section. Then I got to work.

It was loud in the diner. Music pumped through the speakers, and people talked and laughed over the clink of silverware. I loved it there. Every shift I worked was busy and took my mind off my problems.

I took orders, moving back and forth from the kitchen to the bar, balancing heavy trays and clearing tables as the restaurant filled. Energy buzzed through the space, and I barely felt the ache in my lower back as I dropped checks off at several of my tables.

I didn't think about Phoenix's shouty text until I finished my shift and saw ten messages and five missed calls spanning my entire shift. I sent him a message that I had just gotten off work and would try calling from the dorms.

Once home, I changed into pajamas and tried to reach him. When he didn't answer, I put whatever was going on with him out of my mind. I had a paper to write, an art project to finish, and two chapters to read. It was going to be a long night.

Hours later, I jolted awake as phone's alarm blared too close to my head. Drool crusted in the corner of my mouth, and I swear it tasted like something had died there. With blurry eyes, I grabbed water and crackers, my cosmetics bag, and clothes and headed to the bathroom. The morning was all about multitasking. I'd stayed up late last night and fallen asleep only when I couldn't see straight. Everything was done except for a few paragraphs for my lit paper. If I hurried, I could finish and make it to class on time.

I kept my head down, silenced my phone, and got busy. Time flew by. And by some miracle, I made it to class, got everything turned in, then let myself check my phone. *Oh no.* There were so many missed calls and texts from Phoenix.

My phone was still on silent. I fixed that and called him. After several rings, I rolled into voicemail. No one listened to those, so I didn't bother leaving a message. I contemplated driving to his house while I walked to the dorm. When I got there, a hulking man leaned against my door.

I recognized Shane immediately, and there was nothing good about how he glared at me. "What's wrong?" My hand shook as I got my keys out of my bag. *Did something happen to Phoenix?*

He pressed his lips more tightly together and then took the keys from my hand, opened my door, and threw them on my desk after ushering me in.

"Is Phoenix okay?" I glanced at my phone again, but there was nothing new. "We've been playing phone tag since yesterday. I had to work, and—"

"Spare me the details," Shane growled, "and stop playing games with Phoenix. His head's all messed up."

"What are you talking about? I'm not playing games with him."

"He's been calling and texting you because he found out you're pregnant. He's stuck at home, wondering what the fuck is going on and freaking out. You need to do damage control. Tell Phoenix the baby isn't his or something so his fourteen-year-old brain can accept the situation in stages."

"I never told him I'm pregnant. And fuck you for thinking I would." I jabbed my finger into his chest.

"I didn't say you did, just that you need to fix it."

He was such an alpha asshole. I could have kicked myself for letting my guard down so much. That was what Phoenix had been like before the accident, and I needed the reminder that he would most likely return to it when his memories came back— he would be like his brother.

"Thanks so much for your concern and unwarranted accusations." I needed to do something, for sure, but probably not what Shane wanted me to do. "I'm the pregnant one, and I'm dealing with that by myself."

"Just call him back and say whatever you need to, because my brother is losing his shit. He needs to get well before he deals with any of this." He waved his arm at my stomach.

Asshole. "Fine with me." I stomped to the door and held it open. After he'd walked through, I slammed it as hard as I could, wishing I could put an end to this nightmare. I'd told Shane I was okay with Phoenix not knowing.

That was a lie. It wasn't fine at all.

CHAPTER ELEVEN

PHOENIX

Aspen's avoiding me. It pissed me off. All I wanted to know was whether I was going to be a father. And for fuck's sake, at fourteen, nineteen, whatever, I was way too young to be responsible for a kid.

It didn't escape me that I'd told her about my dad and how I would never abandon my kid. In the pool, I did another lap. I was pushing myself past what I should have been doing, and I knew it but couldn't stop. I was going crazy, and not being able to get ahold of Aspen wasn't helping. Finally, Shane picked up after practice and promised to talk to her.

When my phone rang, I hauled myself out of the pool on shaky legs. *Fuck this weak shit. You need to get better and stronger, and you need to do it fast.* I hit the speaker button after answering Shane's call. "Did you talk to her?"

"Yeah, she's going to call. I just left the dorm. I've got to do some more bullshit errands. I just wanted you to know."

"Thanks, man."

No one would tell me if it was true. Worst-case scenarios ran through my mind at breakneck speed. She'd seen the house —maybe she thought our family had money. We did, but it was

Grandad's or Uncle Lucas's. Mom didn't have shit, thanks to my dad leaving her to raise two kids on her own and offering no financial support.

I wished Shane would just be straight with me. I knew he was worried. He'd told me some stuff and alluded to other things that were starting to make a tiny bit of sense. I needed to talk to someone. I was going to lose my mind.

After toweling off, I went inside to the smell of percolating coffee saturating the kitchen and my mom midyawn.

I fell onto the island chair, my legs protesting too much. "Did you know?"

"Did I know what, sweetie?"

"About Aspen and that she's pregnant."

Mom stood up straight, her mouth forming an O.

I had my answer even before she said a word. *Fuck.*

She schooled her expression but saw mine and clearly gave up trying to hide how she felt. "Yes. I found out at the hospital, after the accident. I saw her chart. And there was also a scene with her dad."

"Am I the father?"

"She hasn't told me you are, but… I suspect you might be."

"What happened with her father? No holding back, Mom. Please. I'm losing it, trying to figure all this out."

She gave me a small nod, poured herself a cup of coffee, and brought it with her to the island. She sat in a chair next to me, swiveling so that we faced each other.

"I came in at the end of it, but he was upset about her still being pregnant. I just"—she shrugged—"I don't understand how a parent could hope that their kid miscarries."

"He sounds like an ass." If I'd been awake, I would have shut him up.

"I don't want to make any snap judgements. There was so much stress and fear for those first few days… I doubt he meant it. Or there's more behind his behavior that I'm not privy to."

"It doesn't change what he said."

A sad smile tugged at her mouth. "We all say things at times we don't mean, that we regret. He's human. Don't make any judgements about him until you know everything." She held up a hand. "And I don't know much. I'm just being honest with you about what I do know."

I ran my hands through my hair. The dull hammering in my head wouldn't go away, but at least the pains weren't shooting through my skull anymore. There was nothing I could do about it—about anything. I had to find out if Aspen was pregnant with my baby.

Mom ran a hand over her mouth but dropped it as soon as she noticed me watching her.

"Are you disappointed?"

"Of course not. I'm no angel." She winked. "You already know that I got pregnant with you and Shane when I wasn't married. Things didn't work out for me and your dad, but maybe they will for you and Aspen. I hope so."

"I'm fourteen, Mom. That's—fuck, I'm nineteen. It's so weird."

She squeezed my hand and held on tightly. "I know it's strange. And that's even more reason to take a step back and let yourself get used to the probability that she's pregnant and the possibility that you're the father."

"I know you're right, but I can't stop thinking about her." There was that shooting pain in my left temple. "Why would she lie to me about something like that?"

"Maybe she didn't. You could have known all along. But we all were trying to be careful around you, to give your brain a chance to heal. And it will." She stressed the last part so much that even I believed her, though hope was proving to be fleeting.

"I like Aspen a lot," she said softly. "And from how you've acted around her, it's obvious that you do too. Go easy on her when you two talk." She stood and kissed my forehead. "I have to go to work. Are you going to be okay?"

"Yeah. I'm fine. Promise." I wasn't fine at all, but I didn't want Mom to worry too much, and it seemed like all I did was make her anxious, in one way or another.

I stayed put until I heard her car pull out of the garage. After another ten minutes, I tried to stand, but my legs had had enough. I crashed to the ground, smacking my elbow hard on the wood floor. Breathing through the pain, I lay there alone, furious and helpless.

I knew my legs were done for the night. It astounded me how much brain trauma affected everyday things like walking. But it seemed that brain trauma was my cross to bear, and I was starting to care more about my missing memories than whether or not my legs worked properly—it killed me to think it, but football be damned.

Putting my phone in my pocket had been the only thing I'd done right all day. Practice was over, but Cole and Damon were lifting. There was a small possibility that Shane wasn't. He'd said Grandad was riding his ass and making him do errands for the company. I gave it a shot and called him anyway. After several rings, it went to voicemail. A knock sounded at the door, so I hung up instead of leaving a message.

I didn't want anyone to see me like that—on the floor and fucking helpless.

The knock sounded again. I didn't have a choice if I wanted help, which I needed if I was planning not to spend the night on the floor. "Who is it?"

"Aspen." Her voice was muffled.

I shouted without thinking about it, "Come in." I stayed where I was, not that I had any choice. "I'm in the kitchen."

Her footsteps neared, but I was facing the other way. I couldn't believe I was in that fucking embarrassing situation.

"Oh God. Phoenix!" She dropped to her knees and cradled

my face. Fear leached the color from her hers. "Are you hurt? Should I call an ambulance? Your mom? What happened?"

"What does it look like happened?" I couldn't stop the cruelty in my tone. I was humiliated. "I fell. My legs gave out. It happens."

"Are you hurt?" She jerked her hands away from me, her voice whisper soft. "I don't know what to do."

"Help me to the couch." I shouldn't have asked her to do it. I hauled myself up so I was sitting. It was hard to do, and my arms shook. I'd pushed myself way too hard—lesson learned. I couldn't believe I was going to say what came next, but was no way around it because she was too small—and pregnant—to take my weight. "There's a cane in the hall closet."

Aspen raced out of the kitchen and came back with the stupid cane. I did everything not to use the damn thing, but they insisted when I refused the stupid walker they wanted me to bring home with me. *For fuck's sake, am I nineteen, fourteen, or eighty?*

But it had given me a new appreciation for people who had to use mobility aids. It was humbling for me, to say the least. "Sit on the chair."

"What? Why?"

I glared at her. "I need it to be stable enough that I can use that and the cane to stand. And hold on to the island in case the chair tips," I snapped, but it was out of concern. She weighed nothing, and I didn't want to hurt her… or the baby.

It took a lot of effort to get my legs under me, and Aspen looked like she was about to burst into tears. It only made me angrier. Once I was standing, balancing my weight between the cane and chair, she slipped off it and pressed herself against my side and under my arm. I leaned on the cane as much as I could, not wanting her to have to take my weight, and we hobbled to the couch in the living room.

I lay there, seething. I was mostly mad at myself, but she was there, and she'd lied to me. "You can leave now."

"What? No way. I'm not leaving you."

"Why are you here?"

Her mouth fell open before she got control. Color rushed to her cheeks. Good. I wanted to have it out with her.

"Your brother was at my door when I got back from classes, accusing me of playing games with you and being a giant ass— again. I'm not going anywhere until we get a few things straightened out." She crossed her arms and stood over me, just out of reach.

I ignored the part about Shane. We could get to that later. "Are you pregnant? And is the baby mine?"

"I'm not supposed to say anything to you because of your brain trauma and memory loss, per my private conversation with your doctor. You need to heal and get better. I understand that, but I'm also tired of lying and doing this all by myself. So screw your stupid jerk-off brother and the doctor's orders. They can kiss my ass." She was turning red. "Yes," she shouted. "I'm pregnant."

"Is it because of this?" I made a sweeping motion around the house. "Did you target me because of what you thought I have?" Jillian had said Aspen had trapped me. Deep down, I knew it was bullshit, but I was too goddammed humiliated to stop myself.

"You're an asshole." She whirled around then raced out the front door, making sure to slam it behind her with extra force.

Fuck my life. What else can go wrong?

CHAPTER TWELVE

ASPEN

I thumped my forehead against Phoenix's steering wheel when I got to the dorm's parking lot. He might have been injured, but he was also an unhinged asshole. If he had just kept his big mouth shut, he would have been… "Arrrrgh!" I said out loud. "What the fuck do I see in him except *everything*?"

Maybe I was the unhinged one.

It had to have been a hormonal reaction or something happening because part of his DNA was growing inside me. Otherwise, I would have gotten far away from him. I should have been able to be angry without being swayed by how much I wanted him—how much I *liked* him. And I really wanted him in a powerful, potent way that put him into the I-can't-stop-thinking-about-him category.

I was trying not to dump everything onto my best friend, but I needed to talk to him. I messaged Max and asked if he had time to talk to a crazy person. He sent a laughing emoji and said he'd be right down.

When he got there, I unleashed, mostly about how much I wanted to climb Phoenix like a tree even though he had been a total asshole. I was so confused. Since the accident, he'd been nothing but sweet and open. But then someone—that bitch Jillian—told him about the pregnancy, and he lost his fucking mind.

"You're not crazy, baby girl." Max mussed my hair then stole a few of my ever-present saltines.

I hugged the pillow, pressing it more tightly to my chest, and tried not to hyperventilate. I mirrored my friend's cross-legged position on my bed and took two deep breaths, resisting the urge to scream into the pillow.

"To address your raging hormones." He shoved a cracker into his mouth, and I impatiently waited for him to chew and swallow. "When my sister was pregnant, there were a few months when she would've happily humped a flagpole because her husband was at work. It's normal for your sex drive to be out of control."

"That's not the only problem." I hugged the pillow tighter. "I don't find anyone else nearly as attractive as Phoenix."

"I'm not surprised." He fanned himself dramatically, coaxing a smile from me. "You two are volatile. All that repressed passion. Sparks literally fly off you when you're around each other. Combine that and the hormones, and I'm surprised you haven't ripped each other's clothes off in the middle of the quad."

I laughed. "That would be something to see. Can you imagine Jillian's face? And some of the others she's friends with?"

He chuckled. "That would make it all worth it." Max bopped my nose with an index finger before his smile died and his voice lost the teasing edge. "I'm not a huge Phoenix fan, but from what you've told me, this brain-damaged version of him is softer than he used to be. So I say go for it. If you need to quench your thirst, you should."

I nodded. "It's ridiculous that I haven't already." I rolled my eyes. "It's not like I'll get pregnant again."

Max snickered.

I released some of my grip on the pillow and leaned back a little. "What's going on with you? How did your date with Jaxon go? I can't believe you haven't shared anything with me yet." I smacked him on the leg. Max's cheeks pinked, and I couldn't help but tease. "That good, huh?"

"He's... unexpected." His voice had taken on a dreamy quality that settled my nerves.

"You *like* him."

"Yeah, I do. I just didn't expect how much." His lips turned up at the corners, and he laughed at himself. "We talked about art when we were at dinner. He kept the conversation going, and it was nice because I usually feel that's on me."

"It's your personality. Your charm draws people to you." He smirked, and I swatted at him again. "Seriously."

"We're going out again this weekend." He grinned and looked away. "I like him a lot."

"I'm happy for you."

Max's face lost the dreamy look, and he squeezed one of my hands. "What else happened? I know you're holding back."

I was. I told him about finding Phoenix on the floor and how his legs must have given out. Then I admitted that I'd gone there to talk about the pregnancy and all of the rest.

"He's an asshole."

I pointed at him. "Yep."

"But... hmm." Max looked pained. "I hate to come to his defense. I despise it. However, the guy learned he would be a father while his life is an epic shit-show. Then you found him at a disadvantage, and anyone would be embarrassed not to be able to get up on their own." He nodded. "I'm placing money on utter humiliation as causing a majority of his assholery today. Not that it's right. Don't think I'm going there, but it explains his reaction."

The tension eased from my shoulders, and I hugged Max

because what he said made so much sense. Phoenix was a dominant guy, probably always the strong one. From what I'd observed and heard about him and the rest of his family from the girls, he wasn't used to relying on others. If we could get past him being a jerk—which could be expedited with an apology from him—then maybe we could move on to my more pressing needs. He'd been the one to suggest something like that before with all the are-you-my-girlfriend questions and the kiss… *God, that kiss.*

"Not to change the subject while you're drooling over him in your mind."

I tossed a pillow at his head, laughing.

He caught it and hugged it to his stomach. "How are you doing with your art midterm? We have that exhibit coming up in the library, and I thought you, me, and Jaxon could hole up in that second-floor alcove on the left for our display."

"Oh, I love that. Yes. Definitely. As for how I'm doing… um, not that great. I still have to complete the football triptych. I have the three pictures blown up to go off of, but that's it so far."

"Why don't you paint those at Phoenix's house? It might help you both. He's probably bored out of his mind, and you'll have access to someone who understands the game and can give you more insight that'll transfer to the canvas."

"That's brilliant." I would do it. "Thank you."

Max didn't stay much longer, and I decided to suck it up and drive back to Phoenix's house. I had his very reliable SUV, and the gas card was a nice perk.

My nerves were tied in knots for the entire drive, but other parts were cheering me on. When I got there, the outside of the house looked the same. No extra lights were on, and there were no other cars in the driveway. He'd said his mom was at work and that Shane wasn't stopping by tonight. I hoped that was still the case.

Before I lost my nerve, I parked, shut off the engine, locked his SUV, marched myself up the three front steps, and rang the doorbell. It wasn't long before I heard Phoenix shout, "Come in."

Once inside, I turned the lock on the front door. It wasn't good that it'd been left open, given how weak he felt. I passed the kitchen and found him where I'd left him. The TV was on, and a game was playing. I stood at the room's threshold, suddenly nervous. After a deep breath, I launched into what I needed from him to go further. "What you said to me was wrong, and you were out of line. I didn't deserve the accusations or being yelled at and told to get out."

Phoenix turned off the TV, dropped the remote on the coffee table, then fixed those stormy silver eyes on me.

I held still from his intensity. The room seemed to shrink, and I swore he was doing that thing where he saw into me. I refused to drop his gaze.

"You're right. I'm sorry. It was a shock, and I reacted poorly."

Seriously, this new version of Phoenix was so much nicer. I only wished he would merge the two, and I could like him equally when he got his memories back.

"Come over here, please."

My legs shook as I did as he asked. He was a lot to take in. Gorgeous, even at a disadvantage. Athletic and powerful like a panther, and seemingly relaxed when we both knew he could strike at any moment, moving so quickly that his prey would never stand a chance.

He tugged me down onto the couch with him and rested one hand on my hip. I didn't know what to do.

"When are you due?"

Tears misted my eyes. He'd never asked. "March twentieth."

"You said we met at a party at the cove over the summer?"

I wasn't supposed to tell him any of it, but too bad. I was done following the rules and essentially lying to him when he deserved to know about our daughter. "July. And that was the first and only time we've been together."

His hand tightened on my hip. "I find that hard to believe."

I shrugged. "Yeah, well, we don't always agree, and we don't always get along."

"We do now."

I laughed, which eased some of the tension in my shoulders. "Yeah, things are good between us now."

"Can I…?"

I nodded then took his hand and placed it over the small mound on my stomach.

He blew out a breath. "It's crazy." Then he lifted my shirt enough to see.

I let him, and a tear spilled down my cheek at how gentle and caring he was.

"Do we know what we're having?"

I jerked my head forward in a nod. "A girl."

His eyes jumped to mine, and his pupils dilated. "We're having a daughter?"

I laughed, giving up on holding back the tears. He tugged me to him and wrapped his arms around me. We lay together on the couch, and Phoenix held me to him with one strong arm while keeping the other possessively over my belly. I shifted so one of my legs was on his.

I needed to ask because I really wanted something to happen between us tonight, and I hoped he didn't snap at me again—I would have hated to have to leave. But I would have. "How are you feeling? Your legs?"

"I'm fine." He tensed. "I pushed myself too hard." He sounded frustrated. "And the stress of finding out you were pregnant then not being able to talk to you made everything worse."

I tilted my head back so I could see his face. "How did you find out? Your mom doesn't know that you're the father, and I can't see your cousins telling you. Did Shane?"

"No. This chick Jillian stopped by. She's not your biggest fan."

I snorted. "I'm not hers either. I bet she had a lot of flattering things to say about me. And she and I don't know each other, but she sure as hell wants you."

"She's a clinger. Even though I can't remember my life at nineteen, I can tell you she was not a permanent fixture in it."

"Well, she's pretty sure she was and will be. I doubt you've seen the last of her." I couldn't even be mad about it. Jillian and manipulative girls like her would always be around, waiting in the wings for something to go wrong.

"Why did you come back?" he asked softly.

I closed my eyes briefly. *No secrets. Not anymore.* "I didn't like how things went between us, and… I want you." My entire face went up in flames. I couldn't believe I'd been that direct. A slow grin spread across his mouth, and I frowned. "It's the pregnancy. I can't help it. Stupid hormones."

"I don't care if that's it or not. I've wanted you from the moment I opened my eyes in that stupid hospital."

CHAPTER THIRTEEN

PHOENIX

"I want you," Aspen said.

The words rumbled all the way from the pit of my stomach to make their way past my lips. She closed her eyes, and I cupped her cheek and drew her forward, sliding my hand into the thicket of her hair. She pressed her mouth against mine with a sigh, and our lips parted then came together again. Every nerve ending in my body was on fire, and her hand sliding over my chest made me want her with an intensity that I didn't even know was possible. She moaned, and I deepened the kiss, needing more—needing all of her.

I couldn't get enough of her, the clothes between us a barrier I wanted gone. I was hard enough to pound nails. Images flashed in my mind. The familiarity of how she tasted and felt merged with another time I'd kissed her and touched her. *Holy shit.* I pulled away. Her beautiful blue eyes were dilated, her eyelids half-mast. She looked so goddammed soft. I wanted more, but I had to know if the bits of memory were real. "Were you a virgin that day at the cove?"

"Yes." Her swollen lips twitched at the corners. "But it's not like I can get pregnant again."

I chuckled. It didn't bother me even a little that I'd found out about the baby hours ago, because that only tied me to her, and I wanted that. I eased her shirt up and over her head then paused as emotions swelled in me at the sight of her golden skin, sexy white lace bra, and small swell of her stomach. "You're incredibly beautiful."

Everything faded but Aspen. I grazed the curve of her neck, wanting access to every part of her. "Let's go into the guest bedroom." It was on that floor, so I wouldn't have a problem walking there. I'd rested enough. Aspen made a lot of the stress melt away, which impacted me physically in a positive way.

Our fingers threaded together, energy crackling between us, as we walked hand in hand through the house to my current room. When we got to the bedroom, she took off the rest of her clothes, tossing them to the ground. I couldn't get out of mine quickly enough. She was everything I'd ever dreamed of.

She shivered as I pulled her into my arms. Warm skin met my hands, and I nibbled on her neck, her pulse jumping at my touch. Need surged in me when she arched against me, and I took her mouth in a hungry kiss. When she moaned, I backed us up, breaking the kiss only long enough to get on the bed. I lifted her so that she straddled me.

Her fingers traced over my shoulders, down my chest, and over my abs. With my back to the headboard, I lightly caressed the soft curve of her breasts, the gentle swell of her abdomen, and the contours of her hips, loving every minute of it. I couldn't get enough of her soft skin or how stunning she looked sitting astride me, confident in her nakedness.

Her gaze dropped to my mouth, and she licked her lips. They were plump and glistening, an invitation I couldn't resist.

I kissed her again, exploring her mouth as my fingers teased the softness of the inside of her thighs until I grazed over the wetness of her seam. Groaning, I teased her, spreading her desire to coat her clit then applying gentle pressure in a circular motion. When she bucked against my touch, I eased her forward and positioned myself at her entrance. The wet heat drove me wild, and I urged her to lower until I was fully inside.

A wave of lust tore through me, and I guided her hips so she ground against me. But she took over the rhythm, and I was free to kiss and touch her everywhere. I bent to lavish attention on her pink nipples, taking one in my mouth and swirling my tongue around the stiff peak before releasing it with a soft pop. Her skin was soft. She was so beautiful.

She threaded her arms around my neck, and I ground her against me more quickly until she cried out, her body tightening around mine, and I flipped her onto her back. Her legs automatically went around my waist, and I pounded into her, chasing her orgasm until I moaned as my own tore through me.

Not wanting to crush her, I shifted us so that Aspen lay in my arms with her head on my shoulder and our legs tangled together. What we'd done... it was perfect. She was perfect. I never wanted to let her go, and the baby would ensure we always had a bond. But I wanted everything, and I couldn't help but wonder why we hadn't gotten along before my brains got scrambled in the accident.

Maybe it was a good thing that I didn't know.

The only negative was the slight pain in my head. It wasn't unbearable, and I tried to hide it from her. She would worry, and I didn't want her going anywhere. Images came and went like fragmented pieces of a movie.

I remembered her and the first time we'd had sex. It wasn't anything like what we'd just done. While this time had been frenzied and hot as hell, we had an emotional connection that hadn't been there then. Our first time had been driven by incomparable attraction and combustible lust.

"I remember you." I turned my head and met her wide-eyed gaze.

She pushed up onto an elbow. "You do?"

"Not everything. Bits and pieces. I remember the cove. Seeing you come out of the water. Beads of it glistened off your skin. I wanted you more than my next breath."

"Poetic." Aspen grinned, pink staining her cheeks. "If you had said that to me before the accident, I think I would have fallen over."

I kissed the base of her throat, and she sighed. When I cupped her breast, she arched for me. "You were so wet. So fucking gorgeous." I wanted her all over again, but I needed to be in control this time. "When you touched me, I almost came right there. I've never wanted anyone that much in my life."

She whimpered, and I flipped her underneath me. Her legs wrapped around me, and I settled against her entrance, still hard.

I wasn't sure whether my body would hold out or give up and betray me, which meant I needed to make sure I imprinted myself in more than just her body. I wanted her mind and her heart too.

She tilted her hips, and I slid inside. There was nothing better than that—than her.

We moved together as if we were made for one another. Every kiss and caress sparked desire until we both breathed heavily and she writhed beneath me. I slipped my hand between us, careful of her stomach, and whispered, "Come for me, Surfer Girl."

Her body squeezed mine, pulsing around me, and I pushed deeper, once, twice, and then followed her into oblivion.

Fully sated, I rolled onto my side, taking her with me. We let our breathing and heart rates regulate while I traced lazy circles along her back and arm. She splayed a hand on my chest, over my heart, and I felt the connection deep inside me.

"I know you're doing amazing, and you'll recover fully." Her voice was quiet, and she tilted her head so our eyes met and held. "But what would you do if you couldn't play football?"

"First of all, that's never going to happen."

She laughed. "Okay, not really what I meant. But let's say later, when you're old and can't play. What then?"

I shrugged one shoulder. "I love the sport and can't imagine not having football in my life in one way or another. I would probably go into sports commentary, where I could use my analytical and visionary skills."

"I love that. You should also talk to your advisor about it to figure out if there is a major for that. I think you told me you were undecided once."

It was a good idea. I would follow up on that when things got back to normal, which I hoped would be soon, but also, I loved the time I had with her now.

We lay there for a while longer until we both decided to get cleaned up. While Aspen was in the bathroom, I grabbed my sweatpants and pulled them on. I was going for my shirt when a knock sounded at the door. Rather than put it on, I took slow steps to the front door then opened it.

It was Grandad. I wanted to tell him to go away, but he wasn't someone I could talk to like that.

"Phoenix," he muttered gruffly as he entered. "I was worried. Your mom said you were home alone, and I wanted to check to see how you are or if you needed anything."

"I'm good. Much better." I grinned, locking the muscles in my legs so I didn't sway or anything.

A small smile curved his face, softening the lines that bracketed his mouth. "I see you're feeling better. That's good."

I nodded, hoping like crazy that Aspen stayed in the bathroom. I had no idea what he would say to her. He was a bit of a loose cannon. He had strong opinions, even though he meant well. But my relationship with Aspen was progressing, and I wanted a little more time before introducing them. He would love her, but the timing was off. "I'm just going to turn in early. No need to worry about me. And, ah, were you looking for

Shane? He's not home." I stayed by the front door, and we faced each other in the foyer. There was no way I would let him go farther into the house if I could help it.

His bushy white eyebrows rose. "And why would I be looking for Shane?"

"Because he's been working for you."

"On the weekends, mostly."

That fucker. I knew there had been something else that he was keeping from me, even beyond not telling me that I had gotten Aspen pregnant. "I'm kind of tired, and while I appreciate that you stopped by, do you mind if we talk another time?"

"Of course, but I did leave one of my suit jackets here when I came to take care of a few things for your mom while you were in the hospital. It won't take long for me to grab it." He moved around me and went into the family room, where Aspen's shirt and bra lay on the coffee table. "I see you're not alone." His mouth pressed into a tight line, and I felt his disappointment. "I want to talk to you about your situation with that girl."

"You mean Aspen?" He was acting weird, and my protective instincts roared to life. I crossed my arms over my chest, fighting the urge to tell him to leave. I sensed that nothing good was going to come of his visit.

"She's targeting you for the family money. She's like that bastard of a father you and Shane have."

Where the fuck did that come from? He didn't even know her. I was pissed. He had no right to judge her. My dad, sure—Grandad could take his shot. But Aspen was off-limits. He had no right. He kept talking at me instead of to me, when Aspen's voice cut through his messed-up monologue.

"Hey, Phoenix."

We heard her before she reached us, and it shut up my grandad. But, fuck me, I didn't want him anywhere near her until we talked. He'd never intervened in my life before, and I got that the accident probably scared him. He was just looking out for me, but he was going about it all wrong.

"I can't find my bra or shirt. Is it out there?" She breezed into the room, wearing my shirt. It fell to her knees, and when she looked up, horror leached all the color from her face. "I'm sorry. I didn't realize anyone was here."

"You're fine," I spoke before he did. "I'll be just a minute. Do you want to wait in the kitchen?"

Grandad picked up her bra and handed it to her. "You should probably leave, dear."

She nodded, snatched her purse from the coffee table, and rushed out of the room before I could make my weak-as-hell legs move to stop her.

"That was not—"

"You've been in an accident, and her being here tells me more than I need to know. She's taking advantage of you and isn't the kind of girl who will ever amount to anything," Grandad snapped. "I will pay for an abortion. Tell the girl to set it up." He got in my face. "This is your opportunity to fix it. Otherwise, I will."

No one talked back to Grandad. We were supposed to go along with him and let him control everything. But I couldn't. I wanted Aspen and our baby. "No. She and the baby are mine, and you have no right to interfere."

Grandad's eyes narrowed, and he leaned forward, inches separating us. "If you want to be able to go back to school, you'll toe the line and get rid of the girl and that bastard baby."

I fought to stay on my feet as Grandad stormed out of the house. I made it to a chair and collapsed onto it. Grandad was a force, but he'd always been aligned with what I wanted for my life. What had just happened shocked me—he'd been CEO and the man who'd always tried to make sure our family had every-thing we needed.

I had no idea what to do about him, but I wasn't going to give in about Aspen or our baby.

CHAPTER FOURTEEN

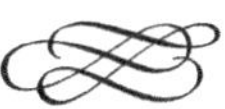

ASPEN

y head rested against the steering wheel. I was beyond
embarrassed that I'd blurted out, in front of Phoenix's
grandfather, that I'd forgotten my bra. And the way he'd looked
at me... I'd wanted to disappear.

That man, however horrible I found him to be, would be in
my kid's life. I couldn't react in the way I wanted to, which was
to tell him to back off. In truth, I had nothing to be ashamed of.
It was just an awkward situation, one I hoped would be laugh-
able later.

I attempted to slow my racing pulse by counting to ten.
Emotions made everything so much worse than they really
were. Still, I had to calm down before I got on the road. The
front door opened—*oh God*—and Phoenix's grandfather
stormed out while I was still sitting outside the house that he'd
told me to leave. I slumped down and closed my eyes, hoping
and praying that he didn't see me. It was not the impression I
wanted him to have of the mother of his future first great-
grandchild.

A tap sounded on the window, and I opened my eyes. *This is
not my day. Not anymore, anyway.* I pressed the button to roll

down the window as my phone rang. A glance showed that Phoenix was calling.

"I would like to speak to you about my grandson. We could meet tomorrow. When does your last class end?"

"Eleven." I wasn't sure why I answered. I chalked that one up to low blood sugar.

"I believe there's a coffee shop on campus that's quite popular." His gave me closed-lipped smile that didn't reach his eyes. It sent a chill down my spine. "I'll be expecting you after your last class tomorrow."

I nodded, not feeling like I could say no. The guy freaked me out, but he was my soon-to-be-born daughter's great-grandfather.

He walked away, got into his car, and waited. Then the passenger window rolled down, and he surged forward. I lowered my window.

"I'm not leaving until you do. My grandson needs his rest, and you being here isn't helping his situation."

My hands shook until I gripped the steering wheel then pulled forward. The insistent ringing from my phone grated on my frayed nerves. Instead of answering, I exited the circular driveway and onto the street. The old man was on my tail, making sure I left and didn't try to go back in, which was what I really wanted to do, but I drove to campus anyway.

He'd insinuated that I didn't have Phoenix's best interests at heart. I needed to process this situation, and how I would deal with him going forward before I talked to Phoenix, who was currently blowing up my phone.

Between Phoenix's calls and texts, my stomach rumbled loud enough to alert the car in the lane next to me. At a light, I scrolled through my contacts and pressed the button to connect to Max then put the call on speaker.

"Hey, you almost back?" Max's cheerful voice filled the interior of Phoenix's SUV.

I released a breath as a fraction of the tension in my shoulders eased at hearing his voice. "I'm on my way."

A drawer shut with a snap, and I imagined him sitting at his desk, finishing the paper he told me he had to do earlier.

Irritation hummed through me because I was approaching hangry. "I'm going to stop for a sandwich. Want me to bring anything back for you?"

"What kind of question is that?"

"A ridiculous one. I'll get you one. I'm almost there. I'll just come to your room when I get back."

I hit the button to disconnect the call as the light changed. The sub place I had in mind wasn't far, and within minutes, I pulled into the parking lot and headed inside, where the smell of freshly baked bread almost brought about a foodgasm as the overly enthusiastic girl behind the register asked to take my order. I swallowed the sound because that would have been embarrassing.

I placed an order for two subs, chips, and a lemonade then paid. Rather than standing at the counter and watching them while they made the food, I wandered over to one of the booths and sat, dropping my head into my hands.

What the hell had happened tonight? First, that shit-show at my parents'. I was glad they were getting along, but it was completely unnatural, and I was still furious at my dad—with good reason. He owed me an apology, and not one delivered through Mom.

But that didn't even touch the iceberg of weird. *Phoenix's grandfather. What was that about?* A shudder ripped through me at the memory, the coldness of his gaze and demeanor. If he wasn't related by blood to the baby I carried, I would have barely wasted an iota of attention on him then waved a middle-finger salute as I passed by. But the situation was different, and the impression I'd made with him wasn't a good one.

My order was called, and I slammed the door on my thoughts and stood to get the food.

I picked it up, drove the rest of the way back to campus, parked, then headed straight for the stairwell inside that would take me to Max's dorm room, silencing my phone so I could think for a few minutes without feeling like a Ping-Pong ball.

I trudged to Max's door, knocked, and dropped my purse on the floor when he opened it. A pang of guilt hit me because I'd silenced my phone but knew Phoenix was trying to reach me. But I couldn't deal with what had happened, and I knew that was what he wanted to talk about.

The freak-show growl from my stomach had Max cracking up, and I glared at him. I hadn't eaten much at my parents' before I'd gone to see Phoenix and imagined that sex burned a lot of calories.

I held up the bag of food. "I brought subs. I hope that's okay."

"It's food that's not from the cafeteria, so of course it's okay." Max dug around in the bag and pulled everything out. I headed for his bed with my sandwich in hand. "But I do not want crumbs in my bed." He glared at me.

"Fine." I grumbled under my breath about how crappy the night was turning out and changed direction. Max had a single room, but there were still two desks and dressers. I took one of the desks, and he took the other.

"How are you doing with our art midterm?"

I was grateful to talk about anything other than Phoenix or his awful grandfather. "I'm close to finishing. I've got the canvas divided into three sections and everything sketched out for a beach scene with the surfer riding the curl in a triptych of realism, abstract, and nonobjective styles."

He chuckled. "You sound like Professor Potts. Realism in the center?"

"Yep," I said around a rather large bite of sandwich. I flicked a piece of lettuce off my shirt, and Max rolled his eyes. "You?"

"It's over there. The silhouette portraits with hand-lettered typography."

I glanced at his art and had to force myself to swallow so I didn't choke. "Max. Wow. It's fantastic." Words swirled around two male silhouettes in an almost-tribal way, creating a unique pattern combined with seamless illustrations of rainbows, lines, and swirls. It was truly impressive. "You nailed it." I left my sandwich on the desk and threw my arms around him. "I can't tell you how much I love it."

"Thanks." His cheeks pinked. "Jaxon and I worked on our projects this afternoon, and he finished his too."

I settled back into my seat but didn't pick up my sandwich right away. "Things are headed in the right direction with you guys?"

"They are." He smiled, but it quickly fell. "What happened today? You look amazing and also like hell, which is an unusual combination."

That summed it up perfectly because I felt the same way. I filled him in on how Phoenix and I had talked, how incredible he was, and that I couldn't have asked for anything to go differently until that shit with his grandfather. I spilled about how creepy the guy was, the bra incident, him asking me to leave, and the talk he wanted to have with me tomorrow.

"That's not good." Max's expression was stricken. "Do not meet with him. Nothing good can come from that."

I squinted at him. "The man will be my baby's great-grandfather. I'm not sure if blowing him off is in my best interest."

"Sweetie"—he leaned forward and grabbed both of my hands —"I see doom everywhere with this. Do not go."

I nodded absently. I had a lot to think about, and after we ate, I returned to my room to try to sort out my feelings and options. My phone was vibrating like crazy, and I couldn't ignore it any longer. With dread, I read through a ton of apologies from Phoenix and requests to call him, saying he wanted to talk to me.

My fingers hovered over the screen as I tried to think of something to say. As I was typing and deleting, Mom called. I answered, taking the escape from agonizing over what to say to Phoenix. "Hi, Mom."

"Hi, honey. How are you feeling?"

There was an odd note in her voice, and I braced myself for whatever she was going to tell me. "Fine."

"Good. Good. I have some bad news. Your father has been having some trouble at his job."

"What happened?"

"I don't think anything much. He hasn't said what exactly, just that there are some issues. I wanted to let you know because he was so distant and I know you thought it had to do with you. It doesn't. Just… give him the benefit of the doubt right now, okay?"

"Sure, Mom." I let my head thunk back into the wall then tugged my comforter over my legs. It was too much to deal with. My mind spun from the night's events, and I barely listened. By the time I hung up, I didn't even remember the rest of the call. Unable to face more bad news, I kept my phone silent and burrowed under the blankets.

I was screwed, and I knew it had to do with Phoenix's grandfather—who, for whatever reason, seemed to hate me especially after finding me there with his grandson after sex.

I had no idea what I was going to do. If the problems Dad was having would result in him losing his job, that would mean no more health insurance for me. And I had no idea how many thousands of dollars it would be to have a baby. The ultrasounds alone had to cost a fortune.

I spent the night tossing and turning, trying to come up with a solution. There was nothing. I was well and truly screwed.

When morning came, I went to classes like the zombie I was.

After the last one, I skipped the meeting with his grandfather. What could we possibly have to talk about that would be positive? I suspected Max was right. It would be a whole lot of nothing.

I spent a few hours in my room, catching up on homework and trying to get through to Phoenix. I left another message. So far, we hadn't been able to connect.

When a knock sounded at my door, I opened it without thinking then swore my life flashed before my eyes.

Phoenix's grandfather stood in the hallway, his eyebrows lowered and pinched together over those cold, flat eyes.

CHAPTER FIFTEEN

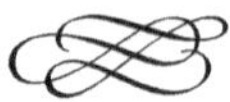

PHOENIX

Aspen still wasn't answering any of my texts or calls, which had me worried. The way Grandad had talked about her and our baby... I couldn't let go of it. I had to get ahead of any damage Grandad could do to the progress she and I had made and figure out what the fuck his problem was.

It was ridiculous that I couldn't drive to see her. There were other options, though, and it was Friday, so Shane didn't have classes and was home. The game was at home the next day, so he wasn't traveling. He could take me to Aspen after we talked because he had some fessing up to do.

Mom and I had eaten breakfast together, and then she'd crashed, needing to sleep for third shift. Not long after she went to bed, I got out of the shower to find my brother playing video games in the family room. I dropped onto the couch next to him, waiting for him to reach a good point to pause as frustration beat in soft staccato against my temples. I wanted his full attention when I cornered him about his lies.

The minutes ticked by, and I checked my phone far too many times. Once his game ended, I grabbed the controller from his hand before he could start another.

"What the hell, man?" Angry blue eyes met mine.

I glared at my brother. We looked so alike but so different, and those differences weighed on me. "Why did you lie to me about working for Grandad?"

"What are you talking about?"

"You weren't around the other night because you said you had work to do for him. I've already talked to Grandad. Stop lying to me."

Shane turned so we faced each other on the couch, and his grimace made him look guilty as hell. "I am doing too much for Grandad, and it's hell. So if he told you otherwise, he's full of shit. I don't know what the deal is, but he's extra demanding lately."

"Get to the point." I was losing my patience fast. "You're my brother—*my twin*—and you're keeping way too much shit from me. It's not sitting right. You need to tell me what's going on."

"I know." Something that sounded like resignation or even devastation replaced the anger and frustration in his voice. "You've been in recovery mode, and none of us wanted to do anything to set you back. And this… I know how you'll react."

"I know about Aspen and the baby. Do you see any problems resulting from that? I'm here. Not back in the hospital. Stop treating me like I can't handle anything without having a relapse."

"Did she tell you?" He clenched his fists and pressed them into the leather couch.

I narrowed my eyes at him. The tension between him and Aspen hadn't escaped my notice—I noticed all of those little things they said or didn't say. "No. Some chick named Jillian showed up and tried to feed me a bunch of lies."

Shane's laugh was dark. "She's your stage-five clinger."

I'd already sensed that and wasn't concerned. She didn't stand a chance. "What's your problem with Aspen?"

"I…" He shook his head and then sighed. "Nothing, really.

She's just there, and everything is so complicated. You lying to Tracey over the summer"—he gave me the finger—"was a dick move."

Pain sliced through my head as the memory slid back into place. That had been happening in small bursts. And despite the mind-numbing headache that heralded these occurrences, I welcomed the return of what I'd lost. It gave me hope.

I shook off the discomfort of remembering. He wasn't lying. I had fucked with his relationship. But with the memory of committing the lie came the reason behind it.

I shrugged. "I'm sure you got me back for it. Grandad knows about Aspen. And Tracey was a leech. You know you're better off without her. But what does your attitude problem have to do with Aspen?"

"Nothing. I don't know." He squeezed his eyes shut then let them pop open. "Hey, wait a minute. I didn't tell Grandad shit."

"I don't remember everything, but I know I wouldn't have told him." My amnesia put me at a considerable disadvantage. "But I never even told Mom, from what she said, and we both know I would tell her before him every day of the week."

"True. He probably did something sneaky."

"I have no doubt. He demanded that I tell Aspen to abort our kid, saying she was trash and I needed to stay away from her."

"Fuck." Shane ran his hands through his hair, making the dark strands stick up at odd angles. "I'll talk to Aspen and iron things out between us. I said some shit to her I shouldn't have."

"What did you say?" I clenched my own fists. I wanted more than anything to go three rounds with him, but that was be stupid. My brain was still oatmeal.

There was that guilty grimace again. "Not too much, just that you weren't worth her time and not marriage material. I think. I don't remember word for word, but something like that."

That wasn't too bad. "What about the other lies, Shane? You

haven't told me why you went missing for months before the accident." More memories were coming back, or maybe I hadn't forgotten feeling abandoned by my twin brother there for a while.

"It's Dad."

No. I stood and started to pace. I couldn't believe it. That asshole had no business trying to get back into our lives. I couldn't even process Shane in the same equation with him. It was a damn good thing that my legs were back because I couldn't sit anymore, not with Shane talking about that piece of shit. "What about him?"

"He was injured in the accident too."

I stilled, looming over him. "What are you talking about?"

"I've been spending a lot of time with Dad, and there are things you should know."

"I don't care about him. The guy abandoned our mom when she was pregnant with us. He didn't give her a dime of child support, and anytime we needed extra money for football that Mom didn't have, we had to kiss Grandad's ass, which is exactly how we ended up here." I swept a hand back and forth.

"Yeah, I know that, but—"

"You had better hurry up and tell me why he was involved in the accident that stole five fucking years from me."

"I brought him to the fight. He was driving."

"There was no way I would have gotten in a car with him. What else aren't you telling me?"

Shane blew out a breath. "After the fight, I was going to tell you everything, but you got mad and tried to punch me. I ducked. You hit Aspen instead."

I stumbled back, and Shane jumped up and wrapped a hand around my arm. I jerked it free, growling. "I'm fine." I couldn't process that I'd hurt her. It was too gut-wrenching. So I decided to go in for the kill on the other issue.

"You need to see Dad," Shane pleaded. "Just listen to his

story, and you'll understand that everything isn't the way we've always been told."

"You're kidding, right? How many times do you need to be reminded that our asshole Dad abandoned Mom when she needed him most?"

"What about what Dad was going through?" my brother shouted.

I snorted. Fuck that. "You're already betraying Mom for the both of us. Why would I make things worse for her? She's the one who stuck around and worked herself to the goddammed bone every night so we had everything we needed."

"I know. Mom's incredible. I'm not trying to belittle anything she's done, but there's more to what happened when he left. And… after. It's a big deal. Trust me."

"Why would I trust you when you kept all this from me for how many months?"

He didn't respond.

I clenched my teeth and forced out a demand to which I didn't really want a reply. "Then tell me about it."

Shane shook his head. "I can't. It's not my story to tell. I promised him that I wouldn't say anything. He wants to explain it to you himself."

"Fine."

"You'll meet with him?" Shane grinned.

I gritted my teeth and nodded. Things wouldn't go the way my brother wanted them to. I would meet with him but only to end this shit once and for all. I would tell our sperm donor to stay away from all of us. No longer would I let my family—the people I loved more than anything in the world—get hurt by him.

"Now that we've got that out of the way"—Shane's features hardened, then he pulled a thick envelope from his back pocket and tossed it at me. "Mark Rowan handed this off to me when he couldn't get it to you because of your coma. Want to tell me what this was all about?"

I opened it to find a stack of cash that only led to more questions. "Fuck if I know."

CHAPTER SIXTEEN

ASPEN

This is bad. I stepped aside so Phoenix's grandfather could enter my dorm room. He must have tracked me down after I ditched the meeting. Max was right. Nothing good could come from speaking with the man alone.

I didn't want to, but I let the door close. Mr. Bennett pulled out my desk chair and motioned for me to sit on the bed so we could face each other. I did as he'd requested but kept my mouth shut. He wanted the chat. I would wait for him to say what he needed to. Then I would air my grievances.

I was beyond annoyed and disturbed by the situation but had to keep my head. Since he came here, I assumed he wanted something from me. In exchange, I would demand that he stay out of my life, and my baby's.

The smile Mr. Bennett gave me chilled to the core. There was something downright evil about him. "You seem to have my grandson's head all clouded by hormones and lust. But I'm confident that when he's thinking clearly again, he'll realize that this baby is the worst thing that could happen to him. It will ruin not only his future but yours as well."

I opened my mouth, but he held up a hand to stop me from

speaking. Knowing he wouldn't listen to me if I didn't let him say his piece, I sat quietly and fumed.

"If you question how detrimental going forward with this pregnancy is rather than terminating it, just ask your father how it's affected his future."

That had to have been the trouble Mom had mentioned with Dad's job. He was well respected at work, which I knew because I'd overheard a few Zoom calls when he had to take meetings at home last year. I couldn't even guess what he'd done. It made my head spin. Besides, Mr. Bennett's threat about Dad's future was no coincidence. "No. I'm not having an abortion. And it's not your choice." It was my choice, and it also wasn't what Phoenix wanted.

"Let me make things clearer for you. I will set you up in another city, complete with an apartment and money for school. All you have to do is break things off with Phoenix and terminate the pregnancy."

"No. Absolutely not." I stood. He was no longer welcome, and I wanted him to understand that. "I've been without money. I know how to get by with very little. I'll be fine. So will my baby." I went to the door and opened it. "And I can't be bought."

"We're not done here." He maintained that arrogant air of his.

"We are. Please leave."

He held firm, trying to use his height to intimidate me. "If you want your father to remain out of trouble and to keep his job, you'll do as I say."

I wanted to scream but held my emotions in check and quietly shut the door, bitterly resigning to having to hear him out for my dad.

"All you have to do is agree. Let Phoenix get his life back."

"Have you discussed this with Phoenix?" He hadn't. I was sure of it.

A smug smile rearranged the wrinkles around his mouth,

and not in a pleasing way. He took his seat again. "Whose idea do you believe this was? When I told Phoenix how easy it was to get rid of his lowdown, no-account father, he thought it would work on you too."

My hand jerked on the doorknob. *Bullshit.* But knowing didn't stop pain from piercing my heart or a strange buzzing from starting in my head. I didn't understand how or why this man would treat me—us—like this.

Mr. Bennett handed me a folded piece of paper. I skimmed it, fighting to keep tears at bay: *I don't want to see you or the kid —Phoenix.*

It was a forgery. I wasn't stupid. But knowing it was fake did nothing to stop the terror that took residence in my heart as I began to understand the lengths the man would go to control his family.

"Everyone makes mistakes, Aspen. What kind of life can you give the baby? You haven't even finished your first year in college. And you shouldn't let one indiscretion ruin both of your lives."

Bile climbed my throat in an acidic burn. I swallowed multiple times, my mouth overflowing with saliva. If I didn't, I would throw up in front of the vile man taking up too much space in my room. I wanted him out because I would be sick whether I wanted to or not.

"I need a day to think about it." There was no way I would take his money. I would figure something out, but my father's job was another story.

"Of course." He stood, towering over me, and I fought the urge to shrink back. "A little word of advice."

My gaze snapped to his for whatever fresh hell he was about to unleash, uncertain whether I could take any more of his nonsense.

"If you mention this to anyone, the deal goes away, and I will keep you in litigation for what my investigative team will find on your father. Embezzlement is a very serious crime, and something like that—stealing from my company—would adversely affect your family, up to and including bankruptcy."

He would plant wrongful evidence on my father? I yanked open the door, holding it like a partial shield in front of my body.

His faded blue eyes, too sharp for a man his age, held mine as he stopped at the threshold. "You have one day. I expect your answer by morning."

I shut the door then rushed to the bathroom I shared with my suitemates. My stomach churned, and I barely got to the toilet before throwing up everything I'd eaten. After cleaning my face and teeth, I crawled into bed and wrapped the blankets around my head, cocooning myself in warmth that didn't penetrate the arctic evil emanating from that dreadful old man.

My phone buzzed, and Max's picture lit up the screen. I couldn't answer. I had way too much to think about. I knew one thing for sure, though—I would not have an abortion. Tears rolled down my face, and I turned into the pillow and sobbed. The stress and horror of the situation were just too much.

How can I tell Phoenix how evil his grandad is? I had been the one to seek Phoenix out, creating the opportunity for the old man to destroy his family, whether or not I could have predicted that outcome. His grandad was full of shit. I knew Phoenix wanted our baby and me, especially after all his talk about not disappearing as his dad had. But that didn't stop a hint of doubt from sliding into my thoughts.

It took several minutes and an almost-complete soaking of my pillowcase for any clarity to return.

Did Phoenix really use me as Mr. Bennett had said? If I was honest with myself, I knew he didn't. Mr. Bennett could easily have convinced me before the accident, but things were different now. This wasn't coming from Phoenix. His grandfather had acted alone.

Not that it mattered. My dad would pay the price if I didn't do something.

CHAPTER SEVENTEEN

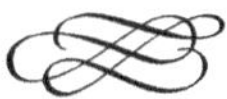

PHOENIX

I t was some bullshit that Shane wanted us to reconcile with our deadbeat-jackass father. I loved my brother, but he was susceptible to being used. Of the two of us, he had the bigger heart. I kept my affections reserved for our very small circle and didn't need or trust outsiders. The day our dad had abandoned our mom, and essentially us, he no longer existed to me.

Fury churned through me as Shane drove us to the hotel where our father was staying. It was the nicest one in town, which only made me angrier. If he could afford that, he could have afforded to send Mom child support for all those years so she didn't have to work so much.

Grandad had always helped financially, but Mom had alluded that his generosity sometimes came with strings, especially after Nona died. We hadn't seen its effects, and Mom wasn't interested in playing games. She was stubborn, independent, and a bit of a rebel, and I knew exactly how hard it had been for her to let him pay for our football camps and equipment.

We pulled into the parking lot, and Shane and I both remained seated and seat belted. "I'm doing this for you," I said quietly, "but I can't make any promises. He left, and as far as I'm concerned, he should remain dead to us."

"Just keep an open mind."

We both stared straight ahead for a few minutes. Shane unbelted and opened his door, but it took me another few seconds to follow suit. I knew I had to get it over with. We entered the hotel and went straight to the bank of elevators. Shane pressed the button for the sixth floor, and once it arrived with a soft ding, we rode in silence.

Shane turned to me when we were in front of the door to room 632. "Listen to what he has to say. Promise me that."

"I already did." Then things would go my way, and he would be gone from our lives for good.

The door opened a few seconds after Shane knocked. I didn't move even when I came face-to-face with a man who had the same eyes as I did, a similar face, and an almost-identical build. Joe Wrenshall had basically been just a sperm donor, and it wasn't as if I hadn't seen him on TV or social media, but looking him in the eye came with a powerful punch to the gut.

The cast on his arm and sling around his neck were new, as were the thin pink scars on his face where the windshield must have cut him. In my opinion, he hadn't suffered enough.

I closed my eyes briefly against the memory of a man lying partially through the shattered windshield and on the hood. Shane was missing, no longer in the passenger seat where he'd been. Nausea cramped my stomach. I didn't want to be there. Images from the accident slammed into me too quickly. I took a deep breath, and when I calmed enough, the memories stopped.

I wasn't ready for them—*not here.*

Shane went into the suite. I couldn't move. Joe looked more like me than did Shane, who had our mom's dark hair and blue eyes.

"Phoenix." Joe stepped aside.

I said nothing as I entered his space but kept him in my sight. "Say what you need to say, then I'm leaving."

"Come in." Joe eyed me warily but with misplaced hope that made my gut churn. "Have a seat. And I'll tell you everything."

I went farther into the room but drew the line at sitting. The visit would be in and out. I wanted nothing from the man and was only there for Shane.

"Okay, then." Joe took a breath and sat on the couch in the small sitting area of his suite. "I never wanted to leave."

I snorted, and Shane glared from where he sat on one of the peninsula's two chairs. Against my better judgment, I kept quiet. I wanted to go off.

"Cece and I moved into the house where you still live, and shortly after, we learned that she was pregnant. Then your grandfather found out." Joe stood, went to the mini fridge, retrieved a small bottle of vodka, emptied it into one of the glasses, and downed it before continuing.

I refused to comment until he had his say. Then it would be my turn.

"I got into some trouble when I was younger. It made getting jobs hard, and before I went to college, I did something to make my record and name disappear."

"Did what? Let's be specific here." If I was going to listen to the guy, he didn't get to keep any secrets.

"Murder. It was self-defense, but it was questionable in the jury's eyes. And the NFL wouldn't have wanted to touch me with a ten-foot pole."

"What was questionable?"

He looked away and then, with a deeply expelled breath, turned back to me. "I stabbed a foster brother nine times and left the scene afterward."

"What the fuck? Why?"

"It doesn't matter now. I was protecting someone else in the house. The brutality of what I did that caused alarm with the law. But with the name change, I got a clean slate and a chance that I wouldn't have had to go into the NFL.

"Your grandfather golfed with a judge who'd presided over my case. They were buddies, and he managed to ferret everything I'd buried from the judge. From what I was told by your grandad, the judge was looking out for him and his family. All the information I thought was gone, he had access to. He's a powerful man. When your mom left the house, he visited me."

"This is where it gets fucked up." Shane shook his head.

Joe grunted. "Your grandfather paid me to leave. He threatened to cut you boys and Cece off if I didn't. I was fine with that. I was new to the NFL, I would make enough to support my family, and Cece was damn sure better off without her controlling and manipulative father in the picture."

He emptied another mini alcohol bottle into the glass, but instead of downing it like a shot, he took a sip then set it on top of the desk. "Then he told me that if I didn't do as he said, everything I'd erased from my past would come out. I would lose my contract with the NFL. No health insurance. Dismal job prospects. Cece and you both would have been tainted. So I did what he asked and left. He promised to make sure you and your mom were taken care of financially but said he would leak all my history if I gave any of you a dime or spilled about our deal."

"If that's true… you took a payout from Grandad. What does that say about you?" I thought he was guilty despite the nagging thoughts about Grandad around what he'd said about Aspen. A chill entered my blood, seeping into my bones. *It can't be true. If it is, what will he do to Aspen and our baby?*

"I didn't." Joe went to his suitcase and unzipped one of the inside pockets. He withdrew a check and handed it to me. "I didn't take the money. Never cashed the check. I've kept it in case you boys came looking for me someday to prove that I left because it was best for your mother."

"Yeah, I don't believe that." I handed the check back. "It was best for you, not our mother. You abandoned her in so many ways. Did you tell her? Talk to her about what her father did so she could be a part of the decision? Because how it sounds to me, if everything you're saying is true, is that you wanted to protect your career. And you couldn't do that if your past met your future, even at the cost of your family."

There was a slight shake of his head and deep sorrow in his too-similar silver eyes. "I was young. But I never stopped loving your mother or you boys."

"I call bullshit. If you truly cared, you would've stayed and fought for us."

"That's naïve. Open your eyes to who your grandfather is and realize this isn't a fair world. The people with money rule. I had barely one foot in the NFL, and he would have taken it away in a second. The damage would have hurt your mom and you boys too."

"So you have a record. Big deal."

"I have a record for murder."

Fuck. Who is this guy? "Then why aren't you still in jail?"

"I was young. Thirteen. And in the foster care system. The details don't matter, it's another life, and I did what I had to survive."

"Does Mom know any of this?"

He shook his head. Shane remained silent, a deep frown on his face. This was a fucking nightmare. "I never married."

He hadn't married Mom either.

"And I lived way below my means to save everything I made that wasn't needed for basic expenses. I did that because I wanted to try to see you boys and Cece someday. And now that you're both nineteen, I thought it might finally be safe."

"If what you're saying is true, he could still come after you with the legal mess." I stood and paced a little in spite of my stupid legs.

"That's why we've been talking about trying to figure a way

out of it." Shane entered the conversation as he moved closer to me.

"Do you believe me?" Joe held my gaze.

I didn't want to. God, I really didn't. He was the villain in every scenario. He wasn't innocent. But if what he said was true, the circumstances were extreme. "I believe part of it." I bared my teeth, speaking through them. "But you fucking left Mom high and dry without telling her the truth. You broke her heart."

"I know—"

"No." I shoved my index finger into his chest, pushing him back a step. "I don't think you do." Blinding pain sliced through my brain, and with it, images brutally bombarded me. The car accident came back in much more clarity than before. My memories were coming too quickly. "You were there, in the car, when we crashed. Driving."

"Yes. I was there." Joe's face contorted in pain. "And I'm so sorry for what happened that night."

"This is too much." I backed up a step and glared at Shane. "I need to go. Now." The dizzying swirl of information made everything speed up and slow down simultaneously. I could see Shane's lips moving as he grabbed my shoulders, his face close to mine, but I couldn't hear him. I felt sick. My memories came at me in an onslaught of flashes. I stumbled back a step, breaking free of his hold. Blackness rimmed the outer edges of my vision, and I thought I would be sick. I was just standing there, but in the next moment, I saw stars.

CHAPTER EIGHTEEN

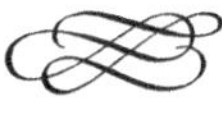

ASPEN

With my phone on speaker, I pulled up the screenshot Sky had texted. My heart beat against my ribs, and my stomach flipped from the sheer thrill of what I looked at.

"Well?" A clicking noise sounded through the speaker.

I could picture Sky impatiently pressing the end of her pen as I looked at the website home-page image she'd sent. "I can't believe it."

She laughed. "I need more feedback than that. What do you like or want to be changed?"

"It's surreal." I pinched the image to enlarge it so I could move it around the screen to see everything she'd done better. "I didn't think the website would come together this fast. And these pictures! They're from when we went to the beach." I had no idea she'd taken so many.

"When we started discussing what you wanted to do with the site, I couldn't help myself. They work for now, right?"

"Yeah, they really do." She'd gotten Riley and me while surfing, even some close-up action shots that were pretty great—they looked professional. "I like what you've done to the home page. The structure and the font." It was crazy to see the site for my surfboard company coming together so quickly. "I think we should do an inquiry page that's a little more specific, though. It needs to outline a nonrefundable deposit for preliminary sketches. I'm not positive on that part." I bit my bottom lip, rolling it between my teeth as I pulled up a search on my laptop for one of the top board companies. "Let me do a little research before we finalize that part."

"Sure. I'll set up the page and maybe a news or blog page too?" Tapping sounded as her fingers flew over the keyboard. "I'm going to look at a few other sites and check out the competition."

I grinned, happy to have her on my side. I'd read a few of her articles for the school paper, which were captivating. I would have to figure out how to pay her for what she was doing.

"I love the idea of a news page. We can have articles or information about surfing competitions." It was something I could play with, and maybe Sky would be willing to write a few.

"I like that too. I'll work on them, and we can reconvene later in the week or next, depending on our school workloads."

When we hung up, I pulled up the home page again, exhilarated by how real it made everything I'd dreamed up for my future feel.

Afterward, I was left with homework and my wandering mind, which kept going back to the problem with Mr. Bennett. I flipped the page in my notebook, skimming my notes in preparation for an upcoming quiz. I would rather have been doing just about anything else.

The knock at my door sent a burst of happiness through me. I threw it open and grinned at Max. I needed a distraction—from homework and the insanity surrounding Phoenix's grandfather and my anxiety about how Phoenix had stopped calling—like my next breath.

Max stood with a perplexed look on his face and his arms

full of art supplies. "The suspense is killing me. What are we doing? What's the secret project you wanted to talk about?"

I grabbed his elbow, pulled him inside, and shut the door behind him. "You know my surfboard?" I waited for him to nod. "I'm going to start a company where I do custom paintings to order and a selection of premade ones."

"So… a surfboard company?" Max set his art box and sketchbook on my desk. "Are you working with a specific company, like the top ones for professional surfers?"

I bit my lower lip. That was the problem. "No. Not yet. But… maybe we can find someone with a background with one of the top companies and make our own? Eventually." I paced the short expanse of my room, liking the idea more as I talked it through with him.

"I'm not trying to burst your bubble"—Max sat on my bed— "but how would you pay this person?"

Damn it, there were always obstacles. I paused by my desk then waved the entire thought away. "Fine. That's for later. I'll table it for when the company is profitable."

"It's a solid plan. If you can get someone who knows what they're doing, you can slide right into being competitive, combining two things you love."

"Right?" I was so excited I could barely contain myself. "I talked with Sky this morning. She's already started building the website and said Damon would help me get all the paperwork done for the LLC and EIN. I will finish that in my spare time, but I need inventory to sell. Which is where you come in."

Max's dark brows furrowed. "I'm sorry, what?"

"I was wondering if you wanted to be a partner in my company. It's a lot. I know." I wrung my hands, energy zinging through me. "My sister is the other partner. We would each own a third. You said you weren't sure what to do with your art degree when we graduate. Would this be something that interests you?" My body was so tense my neck hurt. I wanted Max in my life after graduation. He was an amazing friend. I trusted him.

A slow grin spread across his face. "Yeah, I'm more than interested. But tell me more before I fully commit." He rolled his eyes and laughed. "Okay, we both know I will, but I want to hear more anyway."

"We have very different styles, and that makes sense. It would cater to more people—potential customers. Eventually, we can hire a bigger team, but we're starting with the three of us, and we'll be the sole owners." I resumed my pacing as ideas flooded my mind. "I love what you're doing for your thesis. You have this innovative, edgy talent, and I can see people scrambling to get their hands on an original you created."

"The typography artwork?" He pushed a lock of dark hair off his forehead.

"Yeah, with the silhouette. It's edgy and cool. Plus, there's so much you can do with that. Of course, you can design boards however you want, but I've never seen anything like that on a board before, and you never know." I stopped and caught his eye. "It could blow up."

"Wouldn't that be cool?" Max scooted forward. "We need a contract. And to photograph the completed boards."

"Right. There's so much work to do. Riley mentioned her stepdad is a lawyer, and he might be able to do a reduced rate for a business contract between us. I'll talk to her and find out for sure." I would have to confirm everything, but I was all in if she said it was a go.

"Okay, I'm in."

I squealed and threw myself at him. Max wrapped his arms around me and laughed, the sound loud and rich in my ear. When he released me, I went to grab my art supplies. "Do you have some time today?"

"You had me bring my stuff. I assumed we were going somewhere to work, but I thought it was related to the conflict-and-adversity-themed project."

I shuddered. "I don't want to do that one. I have zero good ideas."

"We can brainstorm later." He glanced around my room. "Are we designing on canvas or paper for the surfboards?"

"I saved up a little money and bought a few used boards that are from reputable brands. It'll take a while to sand them down so the paint adheres to the surface. But before we work on that, I thought we could sketch designs."

"Let's go to the beach. It's the best place for inspiration."

"I love that. I could spend every day there and never get sick of it."

Max grabbed his stuff and some of mine. "Then you're going to have to make this business a success and buy a beach house."

That was the plan. After we stepped out into the hall, I tested my door handle, making sure it locked. "Are you done with classes today?" I'd forgotten to ask. I knew his schedule, but my pregnancy brain was kicking in, and I couldn't remember details.

"I'm good. I have a date tonight, but that's not till later. We've got the rest of the day. What's your sister doing for her part of the company?"

"Remember Regan's in fashion?"

"Yep. But is she designing beachwear, bathing suits, or wet suits? Or something else?"

"Yes to all of the above, I think. We only talked about swimwear, but as far as I'm concerned, she can do whatever she wants." I stopped short, realizing what I'd just said. "But you get a vote too. I'm sorry. I didn't mean to override your input. If you're an equal partner, we all must agree." Shit, I needed to talk to Regan about what I'd just done with Max. I worried my lip for a second before shoving the concern away. Regan wouldn't care. I knew my sister well.

"Nah, I'm good with whatever, as long as she manages the clothes and I only need to focus on what I do or whatever business tasks we divide up, like social media."

"Right." I stowed my stuff in the back seat of my car. Max did the same, and we climbed in and then pulled onto the road that would take us to the beach. "I hadn't thought about some of those things. There's a lot. It's almost overwhelming."

"We can make some lists. It's probably a lot more manageable than you're thinking. The surfing pics are easy. We can take them with you on the board."

"Yeah, but"—I took one hand off the steering wheel and motioned at my belly—"it's clear that I'm pregnant."

"So what?" Max leveled a confused gaze at me. "It'll be perfect. We can have pics of you with a baby on board and then, in a couple of years, with your daughter learning to surf on a custom board too. Or riding the same board with you. It'll be cool."

"I love that. I hadn't thought of doing that, but it also takes the brand in another direction." I pulled into the parking lot, and we climbed out. I grabbed a large blanket I liked to use when I went to the beach to sketch, and Max took the rest of the supplies. "Family-oriented and professional boards. It'll give the company a more well-rounded, wholesome vibe."

It was after lunch, but the sun was still high in the sky, beating down on us and warming our skin. The water sparkled like diamonds. A lazy, warm breeze rustled the pages of my sketchbook and grabbed a few strands of my hair, making them dance around my face. The rhythmic crash of the waves against the shoreline soothed my soul, and soon, my pencil flew across the paper.

After I finished one design, I peeked at Max's work. He had birds in flight soaring across the shape of a surfboard in stark black. Words and symbols swirled around them, creating a unique typographical illustration. I loved it instantly.

The day flew by, and we talked excitedly about plans and designs as we put our sketchpads away. Soon, Sky and I would get the website up and running with the little I had for sale and begin taking custom orders. Ideas swirled through my mind.

I wasn't the only one who surfed. Riley could model some of the boards too. And the director of the art department had agreed that once we were able to transfer our ideas onto the surfboards, I could stow them in a supply closet for students. We would take pictures of the boards on the beach and in the tall grass, carried and alone. The sooner we got to work and took the pictures, we could add to the website's gallery and set up some ads.

Things were moving fast and coming to life. My business had gone from idea to almost reality and had the potential to support both the baby and me.

Back in the dorm, I paused at my door to unlock it. "How are things going with Jaxon?"

Max's eyes sparkled, and a smile of pure joy curved his lips. "So good that I'm worried I'll screw it up."

"Stop." I smacked his arm. "He's lucky to have you." Leaning against the doorjamb and reluctant to go in, I pressed for more info. "What's his family like?"

"I haven't met them yet. He's got a sister, but he was cagey about her, so there's maybe some drama there. I don't know. I didn't want to pry." Max slowly walked backward after checking his phone. "He'll be at my door soon. I've got to run, but thank you for today. I'm excited about our new adventure."

"Me too." Including him in the business felt right, and I knew Regan would be fine with it. I would call her and bring her up to speed. "And I'm sure Jaxon will open up soon. Have fun."

I pushed my door open and checked to see if Phoenix had called. I was so caught up in business ideas and trying to push the problem with his grandfather out of my mind that I hadn't left another message for him. I thought it strange that he hadn't called back after our first round of phone tag. I tried not to read into it, but that was hard. I wondered whether his grandfather had enough influence that he could come between us.

Exhausted from very little sleep and the long day at the beach with Max, I grabbed my phone, flopped onto the chair my friends had gotten me, and called Mom. I didn't care what Mr. Bennett said about not telling anyone. I needed to talk it through.

"Mom." A wave of anxiety washed over me. I knew I sounded panicked.

"What's wrong, Aspen?" Her tone matched mine.

"Possibly everything but hopefully nothing." Everything that I'd successfully suppressed all day rushed to the forefront. Just thinking about what Phoenix's grandfather had threatened me with made me want to hide in my room. *I can survive on saltines and water, right?*

Getting out with Max had helped a lot, but it was time to deal with things, and I needed to include Mom in the mix since the old man had threatened Dad. "Phoenix's grandfather came by today. Dad works for his company. Did you know that?"

"I think your father knows that. Why? It shouldn't matter."

It did, and I told Mom every nasty threat the old man had made. "I don't know what to do. I've ruined things. Dad could lose his job. I'm not supposed to see Phoenix. Then there's the baby—I will *not* get rid of her."

"Her?"

Oh, right. I hadn't told anyone other than Phoenix and Max. "I'm having a little girl." Everything went soft in me for a moment, but then I snapped out of it. "But, Mom, focus. What am I going to do?"

"To be honest, I'm shocked. Is Phoenix anything like his grandfather? Because if he is, you need to stay away from him."

"No. He's nothing like him." I could see a future with him, at least in his current headspace. His nineteen-year-old one drove me crazy. Maybe things could work out if there was a way to combine the two. I wasn't entirely sure.

"I didn't think he was, but we've only interacted with him when we met him during that dinner where you dropped the 'I'm pregnant' bomb on us—in public, mind you."

"Yeah, sorry about that." I should've thought that through a little more.

"Here's what you're going to do. You're going to tell Phoenix what Mr. Bennett said. He's a part of this and should be included in how you deal with his grandfather."

"I was going to, but I needed to talk it through first. What about Dad?"

"Honey, if it comes down to it, your father can get a different job. Don't worry about that."

"What about the litigations and bankruptcy threat? And the insurance?" Mom's job didn't pay enough, and I wasn't sure if they offered benefits.

"That won't happen. Besides"—she snorted—"it's not like we haven't survived with very little money before. Don't let Mr. Bennett control you. Talk to Phoenix. And we will help with the baby in any way we can. Don't let any of that sway your decision."

"Okay." I tapped my foot on the crappy rug I'd bought to make my room feel homier. "It's crazy, though, right?"

"The worst. Wait till your father hears about it."

I sniffed, unable to stop the stupid flow of tears. This was such a clusterfuck.

"Honey, I have to ask… are you positive that Phoenix isn't involved in this? Is it because you love him that you don't see things clearly?"

"No." *Love him?* "I'm positive that those things his grandfather said were a lie, and Phoenix doesn't know anything about it." I sucked in a breath, hiccupping. "I just don't know what to say to Phoenix. He still doesn't have his memory back, and there's a chance he never will."

A loud knock sounded at my door. Then a deep voice yelled my name.

"Mom, I've got to go. I'll call you later."

I disconnected before she could say anything and yanked open the door, ready to let the old geezer have a piece of my mind.

But it was Damon, not Mr. Bennett. He rushed in, grabbed my purse, and threw my shoes on the floor near my feet.

"Come on. We've got to go."

I toed on my shoes, frowning at him. "Where? And why?"

"Phoenix collapsed yesterday. There's a blood clot in his brain, and they rushed him into surgery."

"Oh God." I dropped to my knees, and all the air left my lungs.

Damon cursed under his breath then helped me up. "I'm sorry, Aspen. He's out of surgery. I didn't mean to scare you. I just thought you would want to know and be with him, even though he isn't awake yet."

My hands shook as I grabbed my keys. "Will you take me there?" The thought of losing him—not that he was ever mine—was more than I could handle.

His grandfather was undoubtedly going to be there, but I didn't care. I would go and be by his side, which was all the answer that man needed.

CHAPTER NINETEEN

PHOENIX

Fuck me... why does my head feel like someone took a bat to it? Bright light exploded, amplifying the pain when I opened my eyes. There were too many noises, and each one felt like an ice pick to my brain. Soft murmurs floated about the room behind the too-loud beep of a monitor, and I felt someone holding both of my hands. It was a repeat of what had happened after the accident, and a sense of out-of-control panic filled me.

Breathing through the pain, I waited until some of it faded enough to try to speak without risking throwing up everywhere. But in spite of how much it sucked to be back in the hospital, something good came of it. *I remember everything.*

"Lights." My throat was raw as hell.

"Phoenix?" Mom's soft voice was filled with so much worry.

Someone dimmed the lights, and I attempted to open my eyes again. It was more tolerable. The pain was still there but not excruciating. I took a minute to breathe and let everyone in the room sharpen into focus. Mom was on one side with Aspen on the other, and both held on to me like I was their lifeline.

I relaxed, seeing my brother, cousins, Riley, and Sky, but no

Joe or Grandad. I would have to deal with that situation, but first... "Head hurts."

"I'll get something for your IV, honey," Mom said. "Just a minute."

She released my hand, probably to get the doc. I was surprised to have so many people in the room with me, but Mom had pull. We must have been in the hospital where she worked. Aspen's hand tightened, and I bore the agony of turning so I could see her. Her lower lip quivered, and her eyes were red and puffy.

I was so goddammed glad she was there. After hearing Joe—my dad—out then remembering what Grandad had said about Aspen... there were too many similarities. I only hoped Grandad hadn't gotten to her yet. But he must not have since she was there with me.

"What's going on?" My voice was rough. They'd probably put a tube down my throat again. "Why do you all look like I'm dying?" *Am I dying?*

Mom came back in before they could answer, with the doctor and a nurse in tow. She handed me a cup with ice chips. "This is Dr. Mathias. He performed your procedure, Phoenix." She took my hand in hers again as the nurse moved behind her to access my IV and push meds into the line with a syringe. I willed them to work faster.

"Hello, Phoenix." Dr. Mathias smiled. He was an old guy of average height with kind brown eyes. "Do you remember anything that happened before you woke up?"

Here we go again. At least this time, I had my memory—all of it. "I was at a hotel where Joe and my brother were. I was going to leave, and that's where it ends. I don't remember leaving."

"That's correct. You collapsed, but your brother and Joe caught you. You didn't hit your head. When you were brought here, we discovered you had a brain aneurysm. It hadn't ruptured, which was a very good thing. I was able to perform a noninvasive coiling procedure by making a small incision in the femoral artery in your groin."

He asked questions to test my speech, memory, and physical movement. I was under observation, per the doc, and couldn't leave for a day or two, and he wanted me to lie flat to keep my blood pressure under control.

When the doc left, I addressed Shane. "Keep Joe and Grandad out until tomorrow."

"Got it. I'm sorry, I…"

I knew what my brother thought. "It's not your fault." But I had to deal with Grandad and Joe when I was strong enough. Not while I had to be careful about blood pressure.

Aspen tried to slip her hand from mine, but I tightened my hold. "Stay, please." We had some things to discuss, and I wanted to keep her by my side so she couldn't be ambushed.

"Mom, I need your help with anything Aspen needs. And don't leave her alone." I directed that last part to my brother because he would understand. I wasn't sure Mom knew what Grandad had done to her relationship, and there was no way I would let him sabotage mine.

"Of course, honey." Mom stood and kissed me on the forehead. "You get some rest. We'll go to the waiting room, except Aspen—you stay." A soft smile curved her lips as she looked over at her. "I'll talk to Dr. Mathias about your recovery and come back later. The drugs the nurse gave you may make you sleepy, but the pain will ease."

"Thanks, Mom."

"Stop with the dramatics." Cole came to my side, his arm around Riley.

I grinned, appreciating the lightness. "You both look like shit. Football and diving kicking your asses?"

Riley sucked in a breath then leaned down to kiss my cheek. "Get better. We need you."

"So does the team. McAffrey sucks," Cole growled, "and

Coach looks like he's going to have a stroke half the time."

"I don't need any company in here. Tell him I'll be back and better than ever next season."

Cole's green eyes flashed with emotion. "Get your head out of your ass with the fights, dude. No more of those. We have plans for our futures."

A slow stream of anger went through me at the mention of the fights because I remembered the position Grandad had put me in. "I'm done with that." It was football for me. I wanted to give Aspen and our baby a better life, one where she didn't have to worry about finances or waitressing or if her dad's job was threatened by some asshole old man.

The fights were nothing but a risk. I had to be smarter and get a handle on what Grandad was doing to my family before he took everything away in the name of my brother and me toeing the line, which was utter bullshit in the first place. Mom would lose it if—when—she found out.

"Get better." Damon and Sky were next, and I thanked them for being there.

The worry reflected in their eyes disturbed me. My predicament was taking its toll on everyone I loved. Guilt was written all over Shane's drawn features.

"I'm not mad at you, but I'm not ready to deal with Joe yet. And Grandad… he's a problem. We need to handle him, just not today."

"Yeah, he's out of control." Shane glanced at Aspen. "I'm going to take care of talking to your teachers and Coach and give them an update on everything." He patted my shoulder then left the room.

Once everyone was gone, I turned enough that I could easily see Aspen.

Tears filled her eyes then spilled over, running down her cheeks. "You scared me."

"I'm not going anywhere."

"I'm sorry I didn't answer all your calls and texts." Her voice cracked, and she had to take a calming breath. "There are things we need to talk about that I have to tell you. Just… when you're better."

"Stay here. I need to know you're safe. And we do have a lot to talk about. I don't want my grandfather anywhere near you, and I'm sorry for what happened when he walked in on us. I'll handle him. Please trust me."

I could feel the drugs taking effect, and my eyelids grew heavy. I fought it for as long as I could. My biggest fear was that she would be gone when I woke up.

The room was light, and noise filtered in from the hallway. It had to be morning. Mom had checked on me several times during the night, right on the heels of the regular nurse taking my vitals. Getting a good night's sleep in the hospital was impossible, given the constant poking and prodding.

Each time they'd woken me, I'd looked over to see Aspen curled up on a chair that extended to a small bed. It was enough for her. Mom had brought a pillow and also draped a blanket over her.

"Good morning," Mom whispered as she returned to my room. "Dr. Mathias wants to run another scan."

"Is this the last one?" I was so tired of everything. I wanted to focus on getting back into shape and football. Because I'd realized something: I didn't want to wait until I graduated. I needed to get into the NFL in my junior year. I would talk to Stan, my advisor, about how to fast-track a degree in communications and sports analytics. Maybe it was possible—I could do some online classes senior year so I would be free to pursue my career.

Aspen and I needed to change our circumstances and make

sure Grandad had zero influence. Worst-case scenario, I could go to Uncle Lucas, Cole and Damon's dad. He would help us. I was sure of it, even if Grandad had cautioned him to stay out of our finances, which was my guess.

There had to be other options. I just needed to find them. And for the first time since the accident—no, in my whole life— I felt like I was thinking clearly about the bigger picture.

Mom hung back in my room in case Aspen woke. She was passed out. It was hard not to go to her, pick her up, and tuck her into my side. I wanted to sleep next to her every night. Even the slight distance bothered me.

They took me for the scan, which took less than an hour and showed the doctor what he wanted to see. When I was brought back, they wanted me to remain lying down until they read the results. Mom said there was a rush on the test and that we would get the results within the hour. She had serious pull at the hospital and was obviously liked and respected. But I already knew that.

Back in the room, alone with Aspen, I dozed on and off until Mom and Dr. Mathias entered. Aspen's eyes opened when he spoke, and she sat up, looking gorgeous with her messy blond hair that always reminded me of surfing and the beach because of the natural platinum and gold sun-streaks.

"The coiling procedure worked," Dr. Mathias said, and I glanced at Mom's relieved face to make sure. "If there are no complications today, and I expect none, you can go home first thing in the morning. Recovery is about a week. You may expe-rience some headaches or discomfort and gradually return to normal activities after the week is through." He paused, narrowing his eyes as he took in all of me. "I mean it. No lifting and nothing strenuous." He glanced at Aspen. "You need a full recovery. You're too young, and I don't want to see you back here until your follow-up scans in six months."

Mom asked questions, and I let her handle it. She was fully

capable of monitoring me at home. If I hadn't been staying with Mom, I would have made sure she had access to all of my medical records anyway, even though I was over eighteen. Shane and I both did that.

After the doc left, so did Mom. She had to get some sleep before her shift tonight. Shane and my cousins would be by after classes and practice, but Aspen was staying.

"Good morning." She smiled and sat in the chair close to my recently inclined bed.

"Morning. Thank you for staying."

"Yeah, of course." She tucked some hair behind her ear, suddenly looking nervous.

"I remember everything, Aspen."

Her mouth fell open briefly before she snapped it closed.

"It's weird, though. I have two sets of memories of you, and they're kind of disconnected."

She shook her head, eyes wide. "I'm sure they're very different. You and I did not get along before the accident. But after…" A soft smile curved her perfect lips. "We did. You were kind, not defensive. And because of how you treated me, I thought I should try to work past my defensiveness too."

"Things are very different now. I can see our relationship from another angle than before, when I couldn't let you in. A lot of family drama molded my perspective."

"I get that. Same here."

I took her hand in mine. "I know. We need to work through it together because I want more than a separated relationship with only co-parenting for our daughter."

She closed her eyes briefly and took a deep breath but didn't meet my gaze. Something was wrong.

"Did my grandfather get to you?"

"He did."

I didn't like how she seemed to brace herself. Whatever she had to say would be heavy, but I was determined to work through it. Before, I would have walked away, but I wasn't the same person. I flexed my jaw and reached for her hand.

"He told me that you didn't want the baby and asked me to get rid of the problem the way he did with your dad—he said he would give me money. Said it was your idea, what you wanted."

"He's a bastard. That is not what I want. You know that, right?" I squeezed her hand, hoping to impress my desire to stand by her and our daughter.

She hesitated but nodded.

"What else did he say?"

"He threatened to fire or frame my father, which means I won't have health insurance through him for the baby. And even worse for my dad. He said that if I tell anyone, the option is off the table and he'll bankrupt my family."

Goddammit. I inhaled slowly, working to control my blood pressure. I was furious that he'd gotten to her and could only imagine the fucked-up things he'd said. "I'm going to fucking kill him."

"I'm not taking the money. And there is no way he can make me get rid of our baby. I think it's too late to do that even if I hadn't already made up my mind." Tears misted her eyes, and she shrugged. "I wouldn't do it. I love her."

I was done. This shit would end here and now. I pressed the call button. One of the nurses walked in. "Can you please check to see if my grandfather is in the waiting room?"

"Did you want him to come in if he is?"

"Yes."

Aspen tensed beside me.

I squeezed her hand. "I need to get this handled now."

A few minutes later, the very person I wanted to go head-to-head with stood at the end of my bed, a stern expression on his face. He didn't look in Aspen's direction—of course he didn't. She didn't matter to him. She was a pawn to manipulate and crush.

Cold determination filled me. We were done, but not before I said what I needed to. "I know what you did with Dad and Mom's relationship. The threats and the lies. Mom will find out about it. How do you think she'll react when she does?"

Grandad shook his head, making a *tsk* sound. "There's nothing for her to find out. I saved her from a bad situation, from a criminal."

"Their fight isn't mine. Not yet. But Aspen? She's mine, and you tried to fuck with that. And our child." I made sure he saw the truth of what I was about to say reflected on my face. "You will not interfere ever again. Any decisions regarding my future, hers, or the baby's are for us to manage. You even think of fucking with our lives, and I promise you that will never see any of us again. You'll be dead to us. Mom, Shane, and I will have nothing to do with you. You'll be a stranger if we pass you on the street."

"Are you finished?" He looked unmoved.

"Hardly." He wasn't getting it. I needed to make things crystal clear and in front of Aspen. "You will stop threatening and plotting against Aspen's father." I turned to her, even though my words were for my grandad. They concerned her, and I wanted her to know I meant every word. "As for Aspen and me, I don't know everything that will happen in the future, but I want her in mine, and I want my kid. It may be difficult, and I have some things to work on, but I am determined and not afraid to work hard. I will not let her, our kid, or anyone else down."

My head was killing me, and the monitor was beeping from the rise in my blood pressure. The nurse hurried inside and told my grandad to leave. I would have done that, but I couldn't look away from Aspen. I'd just begun to figure things out, but one thing, I knew with absolute certainty: she and the baby were my future. I just had to convince her that I was hers too.

CHAPTER TWENTY

ASPEN

"I'm sorry I'm not at your art show. I wanted to be there." As I walked into the library with Sky and Riley, Phoenix's deep voice vibrated through my phone's speaker.

"Yeah, no." I swatted Sky's hand away as she tried to open the door for me. "I can manage a door."

"Pfft." Riley hiked the strap of my portfolio higher on her shoulder. "Says the girl who tripped through the cafeteria door earlier today.

"What happened?" Alarm coated Phoenix's voice, and I glared at Riley, who smirked in response. "Cole, go back to school and check on Aspen."

"What? No, don't send Cole here. I tripped. I didn't fall, and Riley and Sky aren't letting me carry anything. Cole being here won't help me."

"Where's Max?"

Phoenix's micromanaging, while sweet, was driving me crazy. "He's already inside with Jaxon. I told him I had help bringing my portfolio and would meet him here." He was getting worked up over nothing. But I got it. He felt out of control, unable to be there with me or return to practice. He still had physio, PT, and acupuncture going on so he could return to practice and games. It wouldn't be long—he was an elite athlete, and recovery was faster due to his physical condition and the sheer force of his will.

"I've gotta go. We're inside now, and I need to set up."

"Send me pictures. And, Aspen…"

"Yeah?" I pointed Riley and Sky upstairs and to the left.

"I'm proud of you."

My heart warmed. It meant so much to me because I knew he meant it. He'd gone into detail about my work with his mom the other night, showing her some pictures he'd taken on his phone of the pieces I'd worked on while we hung out by the pool at her house.

"Thanks." My face flushed, and I quickly said goodbye when I saw Professor Potts threading through the downstairs exhibit, iPad in hand. She tapped in notes and took pictures.

I shoved my phone into my pocket and positioned myself so that Riley and Sky blocked me from the professor's view. "We have to hurry. They've already started judging."

We dashed up the stairs, and I kept a firm grip on the railing. My klutziness was at an all-time high. It was unusual for me and did nothing but irritate me. I knew I would adjust—the only explanation was that the baby must have grown, throwing my center of balance even farther forward. Nothing else made sense.

I barely glanced at the other exhibits as we raced down the stacks and to the alcove where Max and I had chosen to set up earlier this week. It was the perfect space, with a window seat and an area to study away from the main rooms. We used the table to set up the smaller canvases, and easels were strategically placed along the walls.

Riley and Sky unpacked my artwork and helped me set it up along with the cards describing each piece. They whisked my leather portfolio tote bag away just in time then left to check out some of the other work, giving us space.

Max, Jaxon, and I stood to the side as Professor Potts and two other judges swept into our little area.

"Hello, Aspen, Max, and Jaxon." Professor Potts nodded at us before averting her eyes to Jaxon's work.

We returned the greeting and fell silent so she could study the canvas before her. I clasped my hands behind my back, suddenly nervous. As our semester final, this was worth a large portion of our grade.

Part of our project was to do a triptych transformation in watercolor for the first subject and oil for the second subject. The two sets were unrelated. My watercolor series images were of the shoreline before a storm, during it, and after. The other set was a football game. The first piece was an angled close-up depicting the two teams at the line of scrimmage, ready for the snap. I'd captured the determination in their facial features and the ready-to-spring-to-action tension of their bodies. Anticipation and determination vibrated off the canvas.

The second canvas showed the defensive line scrambling to contain the offensive players. The quarterback—Phoenix, of course—had his arm cocked back, ready to launch the ball into the air. I'd tried to capture movement, the players' focused urgency, and their intense drive. It was the beauty of the game, the sheer force of the players as they did the jobs they were there to do.

The final canvas depicted victory after a receiver caught the ball and held it high in the end zone as the team celebrated a win. But it wasn't only about the winning team. The opposition played an equal part in the hard-fought game. Exhaustion, defeat, and disappointment were stamped on many features, and their body language had shifted. The price of playing wasn't always easy.

Those six canvases had taken me days and many, many

hours to complete. I'd worked on the football ones with Phoenix. He'd explained the positions and what the specific players were trying to do in the pictures I'd taken of one of the games. That alone gave me insight I wouldn't have had otherwise, and I'd transferred it onto canvas.

We'd had that assignment the longest, but it wasn't meant to carry the most weight of our final. Those were positioned in the center of the table. I loved Max's typography artwork. It was edgy and exciting. I couldn't wait to see what else he did in that style.

Jaxon favored abstract. I adored his use of color and perspective. We were all very different, but I felt like there were hints here and there in each of our pieces that complemented each other.

Professor Potts nodded to us, and the small smile curving her lips gave me hope for our grades. When she and the other teachers cleared our area, the stiffness in our shoulders visibly relaxed. I laughed as both Max's and Jaxon's dropped about an inch. I was sure mine did too. It was stressful.

"I'm so glad the worst is over." Max swiped at his brow. "And you." He pointed a finger at me while Jaxon's mouth curved in a crooked grin. "You were almost late. I knew I should have escorted you over here."

Jaxon's gaze swung to where a willowy girl with rose-gold hair falling in long waves around her shoulders, lightening toward the ends, stood. The reds in their hair and similar green eyes were enough to connect them as family.

With a wave, Jaxon shifted his focus back to us then leaned down and kissed Max's lips. He made excuses to show his sister around with that soft lilt he sometimes got. We watched silently as his large form took up the aisle, eclipsing his sister from our view.

"Do you know his sister?" She was stunning but standoffish, as she hadn't come by to look at Jaxon's work.

Max shrugged. "No. Jax hasn't introduced me to her yet. He mentioned she's going through something, and that's all I know." He slung his arm around me before dropping his forehead to the top of my head. "Girl, I don't know about you, but I found that judging thing extremely stressful."

"Same. Potts is hard to read. But I'm so glad that portion is over. Now, all we have left is the term paper."

"Why? I was riding the high of being basically done with the class, and you have to bring that up?"

I laughed and lightly shoved him. I knew we should walk around, but I was in the same boat, sort of exhausted from those ten minutes or so when the professors scrutinized our work and took notes. I pulled one of the chairs out from under the table and sat. "Haven't you started on it? I've got the outline done but no research yet."

"No." He laughed, and the nervous excitement had me sitting up and taking notice.

"What's going on?"

"Jax and I've had some serious talks over the past couple of dates." His finger tapped on the table in a fast staccato beat.

Whatever they'd talked about was obviously weighing heavily on his mind. I couldn't imagine it was anything bad. Those two had been joined at the hip lately. "Serious as in exclusivity?"

"Yes." His dark eyes sparkled with happiness, and his tapping ceased. "And he asked me to move in with him this summer."

"Wait. Is he not going back home? Doesn't he live in the dorms too?" *How the heck didn't I know this?*

"He's getting an apartment next year, probably with his sister. But his parents are loaded, so it'll be big enough that the three of us aren't on top of each other."

I snorted. "So you and Jax aren't always running into his sister?"

"Yeah." He blushed. "Something like that."

I reached over, grabbed his hands, and gave them a quick squeeze. "I'm happy for you. He's a great guy."

Max fell into the seat beside me, a dreamy look on his face. "He's the one."

I scrunched my nose. "It's weird, right? We're only in our first year and have found the people we want to spend our lives with."

He rapped his knuckles on the wood table. "I hope I'm not making a mistake."

"Stop. Just because you're moving in together next year doesn't mean you can't return to the dorms if things don't work out. Or move in with me. That's always an option."

He took a deep breath.

"What about food? If you're in an apartment, there will be a kitchen. You're not getting a meal plan, too, are you?"

He grinned. "No to the meal plan. Besides, I like to cook. That's the least of my problems. I'm a little concerned with the rent, even though Jax said his parents are covering it." He frowned. "I don't feel right about that, and it's an ongoing discussion between us. I want to pay his parents what I pay for my dorm room. That seems fair."

"What if it's less split three ways, though?"

He shook his head. "Oh, baby girl, it won't be. It's in that new high rise on Monroe."

My mouth formed an o. Those places were fancy. "That's not super close to campus."

"Two spaces come with the apartment, and I don't think Jax's sister has a car, but I could be wrong." He pursed his lips for a moment. "It's something else I'll have to find out."

"Have you met his parents? Living together is a big deal."

"Not yet, but it's coming. Jax keeps asking me to go to their house for dinner. So far, I've been able to avoid it, but not for much longer."

"You need to get that over with." I patted his leg. "Especially if he means as much to you as I think."

"I know you're right. I'll do it soon. I think getting through the art exhibit and finishing all the pieces was too much to do in addition to the stress of meeting them."

"That makes a lot of sense."

With his elbow on the table, Max rested his chin on his hand. "I think what's scaring me the most is living in the same space as his sister. I don't know anything about her other than she was his foster sister and then his parents adopted her." He narrowed his eyes. "I think. They don't have the same last name."

I checked my phone. We still had to be there for another hour, and the show ended in two. "You should probably get to know her before fully committing to living with her. What if she's a raging bitch? Or likes to throw parties every weekend?"

"Ugh, can you imagine?"

I smiled because Max wasn't a partier. He was more of a coffeehouse, listen-to-acoustic-guitar-music kind of person. I could do either, but I liked the chill vibe better and gravitated toward that with him.

"How's Phoenix doing?"

A sliver of worry wormed into my mostly chill frame of mind. "He's doing well. I just can't believe everything he's gone through lately."

"Yeah, that aneurysm was unreal. But he's okay? No worries from the docs?"

"He's good. It's just shaken me. He's so strong and larger than life. I've seen him in so many stages lately, and I feel like I have whiplash from it all."

"But he's a fighter." Max bopped my nose. "And before you know it, he'll be back on that football field."

"He will. The strides he's made for recovery are so far ahead of schedule already. It won't be long before he works out with the team during the off-season and watches film all the time. I'll see less of him, and I've gotten used to having him around."

"Don't forget everything you've got on your plate too. The baby, the business you're building, school…"

"I know. And we'll find time to come together through both of our schedules. We have to." I shrugged. "Plus, there's child-care. He's determined to do his share."

"It'll be limited, though. You know that, right?" He pressed his lips into a straight line. "He's making a run for the NFL, which means long hours at the stadium, practicing, watching film, working out, and striving to improve himself."

I understood what it took to be an elite athlete. As it was, football took up about forty hours of his time when he was at school. And that didn't include classes and homework. "Yep. I swear it feels like the universe is trying to pull us apart sometimes."

"Or test you." Max winked. "Don't get discouraged. There'll be lots of bumps in the road. Show the universe what you're made of. Go after what you want."

I laughed. "You're crazy. You know that? And shouldn't you be taking your own advice? A certain apartment with your boyfriend and his sister comes to mind."

"Yeah, I'm just going to need lots of moments with you when I struggle with having his sister there."

"You never know. You may like her."

"Debatable. Jaxon hasn't brought her around, and she didn't even come over here while I was here."

It wasn't a good sign, but I didn't want him to be discouraged. "Then ask him about it when you guys are alone. There has to be an explanation."

"You're right." He ran his hands through his hair, disheveling the dark strands. "I see Riley and Sky heading over here."

They'd paused by another student's display and were talking

to them, so I guessed I had a little more time until I joined them and walked around too.

"I'm going to take a stroll around the library to see what everyone else has done." Max echoed my thoughts. "Want to go with?"

My phone pinged, and I caught sight of Phoenix's name. "In a minute. I'll catch up with you after I take a few pictures." I waved my phone so he could see who they were for. "And don't force an introduction. Give him space with her for today."

He snorted and rolled his eyes. "Fine. But hurry up. I'll go slow so you can catch up, especially if you don't want me to do something self-sabotaging."

I laughed. "Okay. No more than five minutes, and I'll find you."

When he left, I took a few pictures, one distance shot so he could see how everything was set up and then a few close-ups.

Instead of texting me back, he called. I picked up on the first ring.

"Hey."

"Aspen, your artwork looks amazing. I'm so goddammed proud of you. And I hate that I'm not there by your side."

Everything in me went soft. I loved how supportive he was, a happy byproduct of the accident for both of us. Before, I hadn't tried to make things work between us either. I couldn't lay all the blame on him. A majority of it, yes, because he did have a tendency to be an asshole, but as we'd gotten to know each other without our defenses, I no longer categorized him that way. I'd been integrated into his inner circle, the people he would do anything for. It was heady stuff. "Thanks. And don't even think that way. You're still in recovery from the procedure. I don't want anything else happening to you." I could hear the TV in the background and Cole cheering at whatever game they were watching.

"Come over tonight." The tone in his voice sent a shiver

through me, and I could imagine what we would be doing. "I miss you."

His mom was cool about me staying over, but it still felt strange. "Things will wrap up here in a few hours, and after I pack up my artwork, I'll head over." It was weird to sleep under the same roof as his mom, but I wasn't going to pass up a chance to fall asleep in his arms. I was seriously addicted to him in the best possible way.

We chatted for another two minutes about what he and Cole were doing and how stir-crazy he was when he wasn't doing what he called his "limited plan" workouts. It wouldn't be long until he returned to school and resumed classes and football. We both looked forward to that, but I enjoyed our time together at his house more than I ever thought I would and worried that we wouldn't have time for that once things got back to normal.

Cole cheered again in the background and distracted Phoenix. I laughed. "Go watch the game." I didn't care what it was. It was sports, and that told me all I needed to know. "I want to catch up with Max, Sky, and Riley and see the rest of the exhibits anyway."

We said our goodbyes, and I hauled myself out of the chair as a group crowded the space. I could see Riley and Sky coming from the other direction, and I threaded through the crowd to meet them then catch up with Max.

I waved to them, wearing a wide smile on my face. No matter how tired I was from the stress of the exhibit and wondering what my final grade would be, the day felt like a turning point. I couldn't wait to see what lay ahead for all of us.

CHAPTER TWENTY-ONE

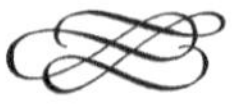

PHOENIX

One month later

I sat across from Coach in his office. The meeting was important, and I needed things to go my way. Coach was a large, bald man. He was the one who'd believed in me the most out of all the other coaches, and I needed to ask for his help.

Grandad wouldn't come around to our way of thinking. He knew best—"the ravings of a lunatic" was what Mom had said, but she agreed that he would eventually get it and stop his insanity.

It bothered me a lot that Grandad was being such a stubborn asshole. If he didn't put the past behind him by the time our baby was born and apologize to Aspen, I would find a way to get through to him and make it happen. I knew how hurt he'd been by the rift with Aunt Linda and her family. He would want to be a part of my daughter's life, and I wanted that, too, minus any controlling tactics. So for the time being, Aspen and I would give him space.

Shane, Mom, and I had a lot of shit to wade through with Joe, and we were making slow progress. It messed with my head that he'd followed every aspect of our lives from afar. Part of me wanted to call bullshit and be done with him, as I had in the past. Instead, I'd promised Shane I would give him a fair chance. He was flawed like the rest of us and hadn't put our family over a shiny career, if it would even have come to that. He should have confided in Mom, but he hadn't, and it had cost him—all of us, really.

But that wasn't my objective today. Nor was the discussion we needed to have about targeting West Coast NFL scouts. My life and career depended on where I got drafted, but so did Aspen's, and I wanted to tip the scales in any way I could. Coach had contacts, and one day soon, I planned to sit down with him and go over my options.

He wouldn't like the other plan I had, but getting drafted early would be best for both my career and my family. I wanted be able to provide everything Aspen, our baby, and Mom could dream of, and I needed to attain that goal sooner rather than later. The risk of injury wasn't something I took for granted, either, and Aspen and I would figure out a financial plan to save as much of my salary as we could in case my career was cut short. I didn't want to entertain that, as the game was such an integral part of my life, but it was important.

But those topics weren't as urgent as what I had to tell him.

The semester was ending, and Aspen couldn't stay in the dorms any longer. I could pay her bill from the money I'd made off the bogus fight, but that wasn't the only problem. I was done with underground fighting, and the money we had left would go fast. Once she went into labor, we would have even more bills. I toyed with a way to get her under Mom's amazing insurance until I had my own from my dream job.

"Thank you for updating us on your medical progress,

Phoenix," Coach Jones said. "We look forward to a healthy season with you next year."

"Me too. I'm determined to make next year and my third year something this school has never seen."

Coach's eyes sparkled, and a slow grin curved his mouth. "That's what this year was supposed to be about."

"It was. There were extenuating circumstances, as you know. But nothing will stop me. I know what I want, and that's to get drafted in my junior year. I would like to strategize with you about the best way to make that happen." I knew my part, and he was aware that I would give a hundred ten percent, as he'd witnessed it in the last month.

"I'm open to discussing that."

I laughed. Coach knew me well from watching tape and listening to me analyze the game when I was redshirted.

"But there is something we need to discuss. He tapped a pen against his desktop, a deep frown marring his face. "I've heard rumors that some of my players are involved in underground fights."

I said nothing. The mask I'd perfected settled over my features, and my emotions remained in check. Coach studied me, waiting for me to say something, but I wouldn't. Incriminating myself wouldn't do my future any good.

Coach sighed then tossed his pen down. "Are there money issues?"

I had to tread carefully here. "Not immediate ones, no."

"Okay, Phoenix. Let's get to the point here, because I know something's going on with you since you called this meeting. What's it about?"

Good. I needed to get down to what problems would face Aspen and me soon, and I hoped that Coach could help somehow. "My girlfriend is pregnant and can no longer afford to live in the dorms. Are there any strings you could pull to help us?" Silence stretched between us, and Coach's eyes bored into me before he sighed and let his hand fall onto his desk with a thud.

"You're young, so I hesitate to ask this question, especially with the fame you'll be faced with, which can lead many men astray… How serious are you about this girl?"

I didn't flinch, because I meant every word. "Since the accident and all the family drama lately, I've gained perspective. Life is too short, and I want to live it fully, not letting opportunities slip by. Aspen is the one for me. I know it. Fame and greed will not get in the way of what we have together. She's my light, and our kids will be too." Not a single cell in my body had any doubt.

"Okay, kid. There's an option that I could rope into your scholarship. We have limited married housing if you want to go that route."

I pressed the doorbell to the Savage residence. It was strange, as we'd always just gone in, but I wanted to talk to Uncle Lucas, and it felt like the right move. I could hear Raelyn telling Louisa, their housekeeper, that she would get the door. She opened it with a wide smile. Her hair was dyed a rich brown instead of blond, and it threw me for a second because of how much she looked like Riley.

"Phoenix, it's so good to see you. Come in." She held the door wide. "How are you feeling?"

"Great. And thank you for visiting me in the hospital."

"What?" She waved away my thanks. "You're family. Of course we would be there for you." We walked inside, through the kitchen, and down the hallway that led to Lucas's office. She rapped her knuckles against the door. "Lucas mentioned you would be stopping by to talk to him. Go on in."

Raelyn squeezed my arm as she left and headed back the way

we'd come. With a turn and push, I opened the door and entered my uncle's spacious office. Built-in bookcases filled with legal texts lined the wall behind his large desk. There was a discreet bar to the left of the door and a few chairs around a small circular table.

He shut his laptop when I approached his desk, stood, and came around to envelop me in a bear hug. "I'm glad you stopped by. Is everything going okay?" His blue eyes darkened with concern.

"I'm fine. I wanted to talk to you about something going on and get your opinion if you still have time." He ran multiple companies and still practiced law. He rarely had a free block of time, but I knew he tried hard to be available when we needed him.

Uncle Lucas rolled the sleeves of his white dress shirt to his elbows. Sans tie, he looked relaxed as he waved us over to the club chairs in the corner of his office. It was a more casual setting, which I appreciated. Sitting across from him while he was at his desk would have made this more difficult.

"I'm not sure where to start." Grandad was a touchy subject, and I wasn't sure if it would be welcome.

"Why don't you start at the beginning with what brings you here?"

I took things back further than I thought, filling him in about Aspen, how we met, and the baby. Then broached the subject of Grandad. "He mentioned that you were set on going into the NFL until Aunt Linda told you she was expecting."

"That's true. And if you're asking if I regretted giving up on football and pursuing my law degree instead, I don't. But that was my path, and I don't think it should be yours."

"I don't plan on giving up my goals regarding the NFL. My question is more about the present. Grandad has expressed his disappointment with Aspen and me having the baby. He's made a few threats, and I'm concerned about what will happen with childcare so we can finish college. Not always, just when one of us can't be there to watch the baby."

Uncle Lucas took a slow breath and leaned forward to rest his elbows on his knees. "My former wife, your aunt, was a complicated woman. When she told her parents that she was expecting, they didn't take it well. And then when they met me, things spiraled out of control. I'm sure you're wondering why I'm telling you this."

"No. I understand that it probably influences how Grandad is acting toward me."

A sad smile curved his mouth. "It does. To make a long story short, my wife cut her parents out of our lives and forbade contact with their grandchild. When her mom died, her father went into a deep depression for a few months, but Linda continued to refuse to have anything to do with him, and at that point, he felt the same. When he came out of mourning, he poured himself into his company and involved himself deeper in his other daughter's life and yours and Shane's. I suspect he's afraid things won't work out between you and Aspen and it will cause unhappiness or take you away from him."

"Aunt Linda had other problems, though." It seemed so far-fetched for Grandad to have reacted as he had just based on their problems.

"His responses are probably coming from a place of fear. Those were dark times for him and your Nona."

"I'll keep working on helping him to see that we aren't the same and things will be different."

"Good. There's something else you should know." He held my gaze and waited for a beat. "Your grandfather didn't want me to provide for you and your brother, and he made it very clear that was his responsibility and that he didn't want me to take it away from him. The SUVs were his only concession, and it wasn't easy to get him to agree even to that."

"Shane and I appreciated that, but we never expected anything. Between him and Mom, we didn't want for much."

"Right." He pursed his lips then grinned. "Your mom's stubborn."

"Yep. Tell me something I didn't already know." Mom was incredible, but when she set her mind to something, there was no talking her out of it.

"I tried to help her after your dad took off, but she was determined to do everything on her own. She said she didn't want to owe anyone, but that wouldn't have happened. We're family."

"It probably has to do with how smothering Grandad can be."

"I'm sure. But you're an adult now. And going forward, know I will always be there to help you with anything. If that's childcare when your mom or Raelyn and I can't babysit, we will pay for a nanny to help you and Aspen."

"Thank you, I can't tell you how much that means to me —to us."

Uncle Lucas studied me briefly, but I knew he could see through me. He'd always been able to, especially since Cole and I were so similar. "What else is bothering you?"

I filled him in on what Coach had said about married housing. "Would you be able to help Aspen break the lease? And also look over the lease for the other house to make sure we're not taken advantage of?"

"Of course. But there is one thing I want you to promise me will stop."

I shifted in my seat, bracing for what he would say. I honestly had no idea.

"The fights."

Oh, shit. "You know about those?"

He glanced at the ceiling. "I always have. When you were in high school, it was easier for me to control any fallout, if there was any. And Damon, especially, needed an outlet. Not my first choice, but I let it slide. Not anymore. I know Cole is done with them, and I'll talk with Damon, even though he's slowed down. It's your choice whether to talk to Shane yourself, or I will. But they need to stop. You can't risk your career by doing something illegal like that."

I said nothing for a second. He took that as resistance.

"You're an adult. You have a family to support and a future that's bright. Lead by example. The underground scene is not that."

CHAPTER TWENTY-TWO

ASPEN

"I have a plan." Phoenix laced his fingers with mine as we walked into the empty football stadium and out by the field.

"Is it getting into trouble?" I scanned the sidelines, expecting someone to yell at us. "Because I'm not sure we're supposed to be out here."

"Coach knows about it." He released my hand and wrapped his arm around my waist, guiding me to the seats the players used when they weren't on the field during games.

As soon as my butt hit the chair, he pulled my legs over his lap so I could face him. I relaxed into the surprisingly comfortable seat, content to wait for Phoenix to tell me why we were there.

It was a gorgeous evening—a little chilly, so I wore leggings and a cardigan over a Thane University T-shirt. Phoenix soothingly ran his hand over my legs, lulling me into a relaxed state. It was after practice, and only a few groundskeepers were out and about. I imagined the coaching staff was either inside or on their way home.

"When we first hooked up, I was so into you."

"Ah"—my shoulders tensed—"where are you going with this?"

His silver eyes locked on mine, and a shiver tore through me at the intensity I read in the stormy depths. "Give me a sec." He winked. "You were so sexy, and you had this surfer vibe I was so into. But you also scared me because I knew from the first touch that one time with you would never be enough, and I didn't see myself entering willingly into a relationship."

"Unless it was a fake one." I grinned because we'd done that.

He leaned back in the chair, a chilly wind flattening his dark-gray Henley to his stomach and giving me a glimpse of the ridges of his abs.

It never got old. I tucked my hair behind my ears, but a few wispy strands danced in the wind, tickling my face.

"It was needed. Fake dating you was the stepping stone to wanting something real. It scares me to think I could have pushed you away."

"You tried." I bit my bottom lip then released it. "But I did that with you too. It's not like I had the best example of what a relationship should be from my parents." They were still trying to work things out, trying to acknowledge and understand each other's points of view and feelings—something they hadn't done in the past.

"What was it you called me?"

"Mr. One and Done."

His lips twitched at the corners. "It was accurate before you. There hasn't been anyone since our time together at the cove, Aspen. And there won't be anyone else. I never considered the possibility of wanting to be with the same person more than I want a football career."

Oh. That was big. I sat up a little more, wondering where he was going. His wide shoulders eclipsed my view, but all I could see was him anyway.

"I never had any interest in becoming a father. Until you. I never wanted to marry anyone because of how my mom's relationship had gone, and my aunt and uncle's. Until you. And I'd never felt connected to another woman or wanted to do everything I could to provide for someone. Until you."

My eyes misted. I wanted to tell him how I felt, too, but I could barely draw a full breath from the force of emotion his words evoked.

"There's more I need to tell you, but I wanted to clarify a few things about my misconceptions about marriage."

Marriage? My heart pounded against my ribs at an alarming rate.

"I know what I want with you. The accident, even though it was a fucking nightmare, stripped away some of my defenses." His hand curled around my calf, grounding me in the moment. "When I woke up in the hospital, thinking I was a kid, and saw this insanely hot girl who I wanted to keep by my side no matter what, I couldn't believe my luck, despite everything."

"It was so hard. The coma. Seeing you lying there every day. I was scared you wouldn't wake up."

"I think it needed to happen. Many things came to light the night of the crash." He leaned forward, cupping the side of my face with a palm. "And I'm so goddammed sorry I hit you."

"Yeah, that sucked, but it wasn't your fault." If Shane hadn't ducked, my face wouldn't have kissed Phoenix's fist.

"Then the accident. The only good thing that came out of that was that my ego was stripped away enough that I wasn't guarded and defensive. I wanted to get to know you, and I couldn't believe it, but you let me."

"It was a second chance for us. I would have been a fool to let that slip by." And he was so different after the accident. I couldn't resist getting to know him.

"I talked to Coach and told him about the baby and us. He said there's a way we can live in family housing, and my scholarship will cover it."

"What?" I yanked my legs from his lap and sat up straight. "How is that possible?"

"If we got married."

His deep voice, so steady and sure, sounded like a sonic boom in my ears. "Married? I'm sorry." I shook my head. "Did I hear you right?" My hands were suddenly in his, the connection snapping through me like an electrical current.

"We both have a lot of hang-ups about marriage. It wouldn't be perfect. No relationship is." He drew a breath. "And then there's the NFL. If I get drafted, it would mean moving somewhere else. Would you be willing to move with me?"

He made me happy. I trusted and respected him. The drive he had, and his loyalty to those he cared about, resonated with me. "Yes." It was a huge commitment, but I believed we could make it work. Tension eased from his face as if I'd removed a huge weight from his shoulders.

"I'll always listen to your thoughts, feelings, and dreams. I'll be there for you and our baby if you let me."

I nodded once. It was all I was capable of in the moment. He got down on one knee, and I barely held myself back from throwing myself at him.

"We're both driven. It's something we understand about one another. You with surfing and your artwork, and me with football. We have what it takes to make this thing between us great. You're all I ever wanted before I even knew what that was. Marry me, Aspen. Let me have the honor of being your husband."

The tears started. I couldn't hold them back any longer. "It's crazy. Almost reckless." They breached my eyelids and rolled down my cheeks in a river of happiness. "And utterly us. Yes, I'll marry you, Phoenix." Then I launched myself at him. His arms wound around me, and his mouth crashed over mine in a soul-searing kiss.

Our connection was unsurpassed, and I suspected it always

would be. From the moment we'd seen each other at the cove, I'd wanted him. There had been an electrical charge in the air between us, and one touch was all it had taken for everything to fade away until it was only the two of us. I didn't know what the future would hold, but what I had with Phoenix and our baby was beyond my wildest imagination.

CHAPTER TWENTY-THREE

ASPEN

Second Semester

Fiery light spliced across the counter from the sunlight hitting my diamond-channeled wedding band. It was hard to believe Phoenix and I were married. One month after everything happened with his grandfather threatening me and his brain aneurysm, he'd proposed. It was sweet and followed a long discussion about our futures. The business that I was growing with my artwork and custom surfboards was his top priority, and he promised to help me make it happen. I needed a lot of help with lifting the boards because of the pregnancy. Other than that, I was enjoying the way things were progressing.

Phoenix had a plan to get drafted in our third year and to get his bachelor's, eventually, in sports analytics with a minor in communications. His advisor had him on a fast track, and I helped him with anything that involved reading—no more tutor with a crush on him.

I would go with him wherever he was contracted by an NFL team. Ideally, that would be in California, but if not, we would work it out. The good thing was he and his coach had a plan in place to make Phoenix as golden to the California recruiter as possible. I didn't really understand how that would change anything. He was already on everyone's radar. But I had hope, as surfing was drastically important to me and something he was well aware of.

It would be my third year, too, when he planned to go into the draft, and I planned to talk to the art director to see how I could finish my degree remotely if need be.

The ceremony was simple, just a judge and our families present—minus his grandfather, of course. And now, we were moving into the off-campus housing for married students that his coach helped us get.

"Where do you want this?" Riley held up a small hand mixer.

I glanced around the tiny kitchen and decided on the cabinets under the peninsula. "Let's put any mixing bowls or baking things down here." Phoenix and I didn't have much, which was fine. We could both handle cooking. But he had an athletic dining card and had managed to get a regular one like I'd had before for me as well. He still snuck me onto his all the time anyway. It was easier that way, but I suspected I wouldn't want to do that once the baby arrived, because I wouldn't want to take her there. School, my new business, and Phoenix's games would already compete with giving her my undivided attention, and I wanted every opportunity to be with her.

"Are you guys going to move in with us next year?" Riley set the mixer and a large bowl in the lower cabinet.

Cole was purchasing a house not far from campus for all of us to live in while we were at school. He and Damon had money because their dad was a billionaire. And they had trusts, but they weren't accessible until they turned twenty-one. Phoenix and I hadn't talked about it that much.

"We'll have a baby. I'm not sure if that's a good idea." I shrugged. "She could keep you guys up at night, and then everyone would have to be quiet if she napped during the day. And what if you wanted to have a party?" My life wasn't theirs to deal with, and I didn't want anyone to resent us, or the other way around.

Sky laughed. "I am not at all interested in hosting parties. No thanks."

Riley leaned a hip on the counter, holding a stack of plates she'd just unpacked. "We want to be a part of her life, too, and help out." She shrugged. "I thought you realized we're all family. None of us are going anywhere."

It was tempting. "I'll talk to Phoenix about it." It would be great to have so many people involved in our baby's life.

"Take it seriously," Riley said. "If anyone gets drafted early, we may only have a year or two where we're all in the same state together. I don't want to miss out, and I bet no one else does either."

"Yeah," Sky said, "and it takes a village, you know?"

"I didn't think of it like that. Phoenix would want to live with Shane, Cole, and Damon. And you both are like sisters to me." I had to laugh because Regan and I had talked about this very thing the other day. "My sister is jealous. I know she would jump at moving in if she went to school here. With Dane, of course."

"How are they doing?" Sky put the last glass in the cabinet by the sink. We were almost done. Phoenix and I didn't have a ton of stuff.

"She's so excited about moving to New York with Dane. I'm excited for them too. And I would be surprised if they wait until graduating college to get married."

"Aspen," Phoenix called, "where do you want your surfboards to go? I was thinking of putting some wall mounts along this side." He motioned to one of the walls. "We could display them from floor to ceiling."

I pursed my lips. "I like the idea, but we need to get a stepladder. I can't reach the high ones."

"You have me." He bent down and nuzzled my neck. "I don't want you on a ladder. Just tell me anytime you need something, and I'll do it. Besides, we can put the ones you're waiting to sell up higher. I'll help you ship them, so it makes sense."

"Okay." It was exciting. Sky and Damon had handled my new website design. It was up and running, and she was teaching me how to make changes to it, but I was grateful to have their help. Things were progressing smoothly. And Sky's journalism background meant she had connections to photographers. I did, too, through the art department and my major, but it was fun to work with her to create the right look for the site and get the gallery organized in the best way.

Max's idea about documenting my pregnancy by taking pictures of me surfing on our custom boards was genius. We had expecting moms calling and had done interviews with two parenting magazines. Riley posing in some of the pictures would only garner more attention because of her diving career. We had so much fun taking pictures and riding the waves one day that the guys had demanded to be included.

The website blew up, and orders were trickling in. There was a wait for anything commissioned because I had to have the time to complete the order while juggling life. But I wasn't complaining.

Phoenix got to work with the wall mounts, and the surfboards were stacked to the side while Cole and Damon brought in the last of our stuff. After setting a box down, Damon entered the tiny kitchen area, wrapped his arms around Sky, and pulled her back against his chest. "Why does Shane get out of moving you guys in?"

I shrugged because I knew only what Phoenix and Max had

told me. "He's busy. Since their grandfather cut them off, he's been working as a bodyguard for some girl's family."

Damon snorted. "Shane's probably doing much more with her than guarding her body."

"Who is she?" Sky asked.

"All I know is that this girl has a stalker, and her family hired Shane to keep her safe when she's not in class or walking to her car."

Sky's frown was intense, her eyes taking on that hard determined glint they got when she got wind of a story. "Does this have anything to do with Jaxon's sister? The one who came to the art exhibition but didn't come near us? Because I got weird vibes there."

"Maybe?" I racked my brain, trying to remember what Max had said about Jaxon's foster sister. "I think she'll be going to school here this year. There was some drama, so she's starting late."

"Hmm." Sky tapped her bottom lip with her finger. "Could Jaxon's family have hired Shane for her too?"

My mouth formed an O. I could definitely see Shane liking Jaxon's sister—she was gorgeous. Or... helping out. Whatever, either way. "Possibly." We were taking this a bit far, but I couldn't shake the weird feeling I had.

"We may need to do some digging, especially since a stalker, that other girl, and possibly Jax's sister could impact our group," Sky said.

"Our family." Riley's jaw was clenched, and she flicked some of her long chestnut hair over her shoulder. "We're so much more than a group. We stick together, and Max is one of us too."

I blinked a few times, because goddam, how did I get so lucky to be considered part of their family? Max, Sky and Damon, Riley and Cole, and of course Phoenix had come to be people I counted on and loved fiercely. Shane was included, too, but we were still finding our footing because of his shit-tastic behavior toward me.

"I'll see what I can learn from Max, since she's his boyfriend's sister." They were right. We stood together, which meant more information was needed.

For the rest of the afternoon, we got everything situated. It was fun, and I laughed so much my face hurt from smiling. I really liked this group and felt very fortunate to have them in my life.

We ate pizza, they left, and Phoenix and I were alone for the first time in our new apartment.

I took a minute to check out the surfboards he'd hung in the small room off the kitchen.

Phoenix's arms went around me as he pulled me against his chest. He rested his hands over my swollen belly, and I sighed in contentment. "The surfboards look good there. Even the corner near the window where you set up my easel makes me want to get my paints out."

"Someday, I'll have the most amazing studio built for you."

"Oh, yeah?" I grinned and turned in his embrace, wrapping my arms around his neck. "What'll it look like?"

"White walls, so your designs are highlighted and the only color in the room. Floor-to-ceiling windows will line one side with a spectacular view of our backyard, letting in amazing natural light. One wall will have cabinets with all your supplies and a marble counter. And sliding doors will open all the way so you can work outside on the patio if you want."

"Sounds amazing." I brushed his light hair from his forehead and shivered at the determined expression on his chiseled face. "But you know I don't need a lot. This place is perfect because it has you and soon, our baby. What more could I ask for?"

"I want to give you the world, Aspen, like you're giving me." He took one of my hands and rested it on my belly with his, and tears rolled down my cheeks.

"Stop being so sweet." Damned emotions.

He laughed then stepped back but kept my hand in his as he pulled me to the couch. I sat, and he went into the kitchen for a few minutes. I was happy to kick my feet up and rest. It'd been a long day.

Phoenix joined me on the couch with a plate of strawberries and whipped cream in the center.

"What's this?" I scooted closer. I had an insatiable need to have some part of our bodies touching whenever we were near. He never complained and initiated it by lifting my legs into his lap or pulling me tightly against him. I guess it went both ways.

"This is our first date as a married couple."

I laughed. I couldn't have been happier or more content.

CHAPTER TWENTY-FOUR

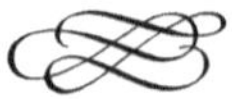

PHOENIX

The alarm jolted me out of sleep, and I stretched my arm to hit snooze so it wouldn't wake Aspen. She slept hard most nights and struggled to wake unless I eased her into the morning. It was my favorite thing to do and also why I set my alarm thirty minutes earlier than I needed to get up to work out with the team. My body was finally back to normal, and though I'd had to take it easy for a while, I was glad to be back in the weight room and running drills.

She used my arm as a pillow, resting a hand over my heart as if she already knew she held it in her palm. I traced the soft curve of her cheek before brushing her hair back from her forehead. I couldn't get enough of her. Aspen was heaven, and I would do anything to stay by her.

I had never felt so lucky, not even when I started my first college game as a freshman. Even football didn't compare to Aspen. She was the most beautiful woman I'd ever seen, and that beauty shone from both inside and out. No one could ever come close.

Our daughter kicked against my side, where Aspen was tucked against me. I flattened my palm against her belly and whispered, "Good morning," to our baby. I still couldn't get over how awesome it was to feel her moving around in there. After another kick, she settled, and I brushed my hand over Aspen's smooth skin, loving every moment of the morning. I couldn't wait for our daughter to be born, but I also took advantage of every second we had alone before I had to share her. I wanted her all to myself and to start her day by feeling loved and cherished.

Aspen shifted, turning so her back was to me, and I chuckled because she was only making it easier, and I knew she loved it when I woke her up this way. I moved to my side so my chest was to her back then slowly slid her panties down, using my foot to hook them when they were at her knees and push them the rest of the way off. I didn't want to disturb her more until I had her right where I wanted her.

Easing her top leg over mine, I slid my hand around her hip and then between her legs. She was so warm and soft. My fingers grazed the apex of her thighs, and my hard cock pushed against her perfect ass. I brushed her hair out of the way then pressed open-mouth kisses along her neck, teasing her closer to waking. I breathed her in, running my nose along her neck, inhaling her scent. A gentle bite over her pulse elicited a sensual moan.

"What are you doing?" She turned her head, and sleepy, hooded blue eyes met mine.

I chuckled, eager to slide into her. "You know what I want."

Her lips parted, and I curled my arm, pulling her head closer, then slanted my mouth over hers, teasing and tasting while my fingers continued to circle and caress all around where she wanted me most. Her hips bucked when I came close to pushing inside, and she released a small growl of frustration into my mouth.

On a good day, Aspen didn't have much patience for games. The pregnancy hormones surging through her body made her horny and impatient. I took it easy on her and traced along her wet, silky slit.

She moaned, and I ground against her, my control perilously close to slipping. "God, I love your ass."

Her heated eyes met mine, and her lips parted. I took advantage and kissed her deeply. The friction increased as she moved against my hand. I tore my lips from her, trailing hungry kisses down her neck and shoulder, then positioned myself to slide inside.

She pushed back, urging me to enter. I slid my fingers along her slit again, circling the tiny nub as I moved deep inside her wet heat. "Christ, Aspen."

Her breath came in short pants as I increased our rhythm. I nipped at her skin, teasing and toying with her clit, building her pleasure until she cried out. Her nails dug into my arm as she gasped then tightened all around me, and I thrust faster, chasing her climax as she writhed in ecstasy.

When a scream tore from her throat, I pumped into her silken heat two more times then followed her, every nerve ending in my body hypersensitive and in tune with the woman I loved. I was addicted—she could bring me to my knees with one look, one touch. Every time with her was incredible. And as we lay together in each other's arms, our breathing slowly regulating, I felt in my whole body how lucky I was to have her in my life. I never wanted to let her go.

And even though it was time for me to get up, I was reluctant to let her out of bed at all, but she slipped from my arms, if only temporarily, to clean up.

She came back to bed, looking like a goddess. Her skin glowed, and her body was toned but soft in all the right places. I loved seeing the swell of our baby.

"I have a few more minutes until I have to get up, so come here."

She grinned then crawled back into bed and my arms,

tangling her legs with mine. "I hope it's always like this." Her smile slipped a little, and worry clouded her blue eyes. "I just worry. We both come from pretty fucked-up relationship examples."

I tipped her chin higher so our eyes met and held because that was some serious shit. I needed to make sure she understood… I thought about making a fucking plaque and putting it over our bed. "We aren't our parents."

She nodded and snuggled against me.

"Aspen, look at me." I waited for her gaze to meet mine again. "We need to make a pact always to encourage each other to achieve our goals through support and friendship. I love you, and I want to give you the world."

She cupped the side of my jaw, her lower lip quivering slightly, her eyes bright with determination. Her spirit matched mine, and together, we would make the whole fucking world our playground.

"I love you too, Phoenix."

We held each other for a few more minutes until my second alarm went off. "Are you going back to sleep?"

"I shouldn't. I have painting to do."

"Will you be outside today? I'll get it set up before I leave."

"Yeah." She grinned. "Thanks."

She made no move to get out of bed when I did. After getting ready, I made her chai tea and set it on the nightstand then nudged her shoulder and whispered that it was there.

She sat up then slid so that the headboard supported her back, looking sleepy but content.

I handed her the tea. "Everything's ready. You just need to put on some clothes first."

She grinned slyly. "I only did that the one time because I knew you were outside."

"And you were damn lucky it was just me, or I'd have to blind whoever was with me."

"Go." She laughed. "You're going to be late."

"Cole is picking me up. I'm leaving the SUV here in case you need it." I did that every chance I could. Her car was a piece of crap, and I didn't want her driving it. I could always get rides to the stadium, so it wasn't a problem. "I'll be back in a couple of hours."

When Cole pulled up to the curb, I left the apartment, locked the door behind me, then spent the next couple of hours doing drills on the field and weight lifting with my cousins. Near the end of the workout, I started to worry about why Shane hadn't shown up. It wasn't like him.

We'd had a couple of weeks off for the holidays, and since we were back, off-season workouts had resumed. Shane and I were taking different classes, I rarely saw him on campus, and we hadn't really talked much. I figured maybe Cole or Damon knew what was going on.

I walked to the parking lot with them. "Any idea why my brother didn't come today? It's not like him to miss workouts."

"No. I thought it was weird too," Damon said. "Let me know when you find out. I'll see you guys later. I'm meeting Sky at Dillon's for lunch."

Aspen used to work at the off-campus diner, but she'd quit before we went on break, and I couldn't have been happier about it. She had more time to spend with our friends and me and to paint, which made her visibly happy, especially when we went to the beach, which we did every chance we had.

Cole dropped me off at the apartment, promising to message me if he heard anything about Shane. I had a bad feeling and couldn't shake it. The need to see Mom was intense, too, for reasons I didn't understand. I felt a heavy weight that I knew was connected to my twin.

"Hey!" Aspen called from the kitchen. "I finished the commission. Max came by to work on one of the orders, so he brought my stuff inside."

"That's fantastic."

The happy expression on her face fell when she saw me. "What's wrong?"

I told her about the feeling I had, and she didn't hesitate. She grabbed her purse and slipped on shoes, and we took off for Mom's.

When we pulled up, two squad cars sat in the driveway, their blue and red lights painting ominous slashes on the front of our house. I went to Aspen's side and helped her out, taking her hand firmly in mine as we approached the front door.

Before we could reach the steps, the door sprang open, and Shane was led out in handcuffs. Our eyes caught and held. A million unsaid words and emotions passed between us. He thought that was it, that he was done for. I didn't know why. But there was no way I would let anything happen to my brother.

Mom followed Shane, and we rushed to her as an officer put him in the back seat of one of the cars.

"What happened?" My gut was tight with dread. Mom wrung her hands, and Aspen pulled her in for a quick hug then held her close.

"Shane got into a fight with Luke Green, whoever that is." Her voice was tight, straining with the obvious effort she was putting into controlling her emotions. "From what Shane told me, it wasn't much of a fight. He punched Luke. Luke fell and hit his head on the bottom step." Tears rolled unchecked down her cheeks, and she shook from the shock setting in. "He's dead. Shane was arrested for murder."

The End

Continue reading the Hidden Valley Elite series to find out
what happens to Shane in Wicked Games:
https://www.islavaughnauthor.com/books

Keep up with Isla's releases by joining her newsletter:
https://bit.ly/IslaVaughnNewsletter
If you enjoyed reading CRUEL LOVE as much as I did writing
it, I hope you'll consider leaving a review.

ABOUT THE AUTHOR

Isla Vaughn is the author of the Hidden Valley Elite series. Her romance books are full of complex characters, strong alpha males, and the fierce women who bring them to their knees. When not writing, she can be found daydreaming about owning a beach house, reading, or drinking too much coffee.

You can find her at:
https://www.islavaughnauthor.com

Subscribe to Isla's newsletter for cover reveals, book announcements, and giveaways: https://bit.ly/IslaVaughnNewsletter

goodreads.com/islavaughn_author

instagram.com/islavaughnauthor

bookbub.com/profile/isla-vaughn

tiktok.com/@islavaughnauthor

twitter.com/IVaughn_Author

facebook.com/author.IslaVaughn